My Congratulations to the

"Presents" Series and to its

Readers —

May the Romance live on!

With my very best wishes

Penny Jordan

Dear Reader,

How thrilling to be twenty-five! Twenty-five is young. Sexy. Sizzling with energy. And yet twenty-five is mature. Powerful. It has come into its own.

This year Harlequin Presents® turns twenty-five, and, as any Presents® reader will tell you, it is definitely all those things!

I fell in love with Presents first as a reader. I adored the intensity, the sophistication, the heart-stopping sensuality. For me, becoming a Presents author was a dream come true.

Twelve books later, my love affair with Presents hasn't faded. I still open each one eagerly, knowing that I'll be transported to irresistible places, introduced to red-hot heroes, inspired by heroines of wit and courage. I still close each book with a satisfied sigh.

Happy birthday, Harlequin Presents. And thanks for all the blissful hours, both in front of the keyboard and behind the pages. May your next twenty-five years be filled with love.

Warmly,

Kathleen O'Brien

# KATHLEEN O'BRIEN

## Trial by Seduction

## Harlequin Books

TORONTO • NEW YORK • LONDON
AMSTERDAM • PARIS • SYDNEY • HAMBURG
STOCKHOLM • ATHENS • TOKYO • MILAN
MADRID • WARSAW • BUDAPEST • AUCKLAND

To the memory of my father, Michael J. O'Brien, who so
loved Florida and its waters. I think of him whenever I
see the Gulf. And whenever I don't.

ISBN 0-373-11958-5

TRIAL BY SEDUCTION

First North American Publication 1998.

Copyright © 1997 by Kathleen O'Brien.

# CHAPTER ONE

IT WAS the last silver hour before dawn, and Mark Connelly did not want to spend it indoors at another of his cousin Edgerton's interminable, idiotic meetings. But he'd skipped the last three meetings, and for the sake of Edgerton's blood pressure, he supposed he ought to show up.

But, damn it, he really wasn't in the mood. He'd been up most of the night. He just wanted to go fishing and forget the whole thing.

No such luck. If he didn't show, Edgerton would probably die of apoplexy, and then Mark would have to run the Moonbird Hotel himself. God forbid. He shuddered at the thought of spending the rest of his life indoors behind a desk. He'd rather ride hungry sharks bareback for a living.

He paused at the door of the hotel bar, his black leather jacket dangling over his shoulder from one hooked forefinger. He took a deep breath and held it, as if he could analyze the room better by smell than by sight. But his eyes were busy, too—scanning, appraising, sizing up the quality of the darkness and the mood of his two cousins who waited inside.

Just last night his girlfriend—ex-girlfriend, he amended—had accused him of entering every room as if it were a minefield. She hadn't been joking—she had been angry, defeated, leaving him. He might have a sophisticated collection of bedroom tricks, she'd said bitterly, but he didn't know a damn thing about real intimacy.

She had been right, of course. She wasn't the first woman who had begun by viewing his emotional inaccessibility as a challenge—and ended cursing it through her tears. But, as he had told her from the first date, he couldn't change.

*Wouldn't*, she had insisted acidly. He *wouldn't* change.

Whichever—did it really matter? Caution was an old friend, and it had served him well. He couldn't shake it now—not even here, at the hotel that had been his home for twenty years. Not even now, when his life had long since ceased to be a war.

Besides, there might be a battle yet this morning. Edgerton and Philip, his cousins and business partners, stood with their backs to him, but he could read the rigidity in the tall man's shoulders, the slight tremor in the shorter man's hands.

Mark swallowed an exasperated sigh. Not dawn yet…could Edgerton already be in a temper? Was Philip already drunk?

They were studying something out on the darkened beach and they didn't hear him come in. As he moved past the huge central aquarium, the strange, bright little fish swarmed toward him in synchronized curiosity. He tapped the glass with his knuckle, an apology for having no food.

Edgerton heard that. He swiveled his head slightly, shot Mark a disapproving glance and tilted his head back to drop a pill into his mouth. Antacids by the fistful.

Poor Edge. Must be tough to be sixty years old at only thirty-five.

"You're late," Edgerton said tightly, chewing with short, irritated snaps.

Mark dropped his jacket on the nearest table and wandered toward the gleaming teak bar. "Sorry, boss," he said politely, leaning over to extricate a bottle of spring water. "I didn't notice you'd installed a time clock."

Edgerton snorted. Boss indeed, the snort said. They both knew better. "You don't have on a suit, either, damn it. You knew I wanted you to wear a suit. You look like a—" he fumbled for a word "—a hoodlum movie star."

Mark twisted off the cap and drank deeply, the water sparkling in the light from the fish tank. "Gosh," he said, drying his upper lip with the back of his hand, "I must have missed your memo on the dress code, too."

Philip turned around for the first time and patted Edgerton's arm consolingly. Though Philip was younger, his expression sweeter, anyone could have known the two were brothers. They shared the same blond-over-blue surfer good looks.

Mark, on the other hand, had hair so black even the Florida sun couldn't bleach it. *He's the Connelly cousin*, people had observed sotto voce, watching as the three boys roamed wild over their tropical island. *The poor relation. You know the story. So sad.*

"Give it up, Edge," Philip said, smiling the crooked smile that was his hallmark. "Everything's under control. Besides, Mark doesn't own a suit, and you know it. So what? He'll charm the socks right off every female guest in the place anyhow."

Mark grinned back. "I think that's what Edgerton's afraid of."

Edgerton adjusted his tie irritably, but Philip wiggled his eyebrows and cocked his head toward the window. "Speaking of which…Edge and I were just trying to decide how long it would take you to part this particular specimen from her bikini."

Edgerton sputtered. "I was *not*—"

"Well, *I* was." Philip moved to make room. "Come see. I know you don't usually hunt beach bunnies, but this one is…well, she's different. Kind of a cross between a librarian and a lollipop."

"Oh, for God's sake." Edgerton's voice sharpened, and he stalked away from the window. "We've got three hours—*three hours*—before this hotel is overrun with people. Reporters. Critics. Politicians. Opinion-shapers. Not to mention about a hundred paying guests. Do you think you can get your mind off women long enough to help me here?"

Philip ignored him as usual, but Mark, sensing that Edgerton was about to overload his circuits, grabbed another bottled water and ambled toward the two men. "Here," he said, handing the drink to Edgerton. "See if this will put the fire out."

He joined Philip at the window and peered into the silver mist.

"Show me," he said cooperatively, though he didn't really expect to see anything of interest. Philip's taste in women ran to the type whose IQs were as skimpy as their bathing suits. Unfortunately, Mark required more than a D-cup to engage his attention. In fact, he couldn't imagine *what* it would take to interest him anymore.…

"Darn, she's moved out of the light." Philip sighed,

and Mark's jaw tightened at the whiff of blended whiskey that floated over him. God—Philip was really tossing it back.

Somehow Mark fought down his annoyance, trying to feel sympathetic. Edgerton's plans for today's grand reopening festivities were a maze of social and political intricacies. Philip was probably scared blue. But why, just once, couldn't he think of some less destructive way to stiffen his spine?

"Wait—yeah, there she is, just beyond the light now, heading for the water." Philip clutched his cousin's forearm. "Oh, my God, look—she's taken off her shoes."

"Easy boy," Mark said calmly. "You *have* seen feet before."

But as his gaze focused on the woman's slim figure, his carefully cultivated cynicism began to peel away like an old coat of paint under a bright sun.

By God, this wasn't just another of Philip's over-endowed bimbos. This one actually *was* different. She was…beautiful.

Yet it was so much more than that. *Beautiful* wasn't enough to account for this tightening of his gut, this startling sense of recognition. No, it wasn't just beauty—it wasn't even the way the wind blew her white shirt back against her breasts, outlining their feminine swell with a curve of silver mist. Bathing beauties were as common on Moonbird Key as coquina—his eyes saw them, but they had long since lost the power to stir him.

So what was it? What kept him here at the window as silent as an awestruck schoolboy? He let his shoulder drop to rest against the wall, trying to affect a casual air while he studied the vision before him, trying to pinpoint the difference.

Her hands were clasped demurely behind her back, dangling white sandals, and her shoulders were bravely squared. She had reached the water's edge now, and as the incoming waves licked at her toes she cast one last look back at the hotel, seemingly watching for someone.

Philip was still chattering stupidly. "Was I right or what? Isn't she a babe?" His tone was proprietorial, as if he had not just discovered but actually invented her.

A babe? Perhaps... Mark nodded mutely. She was so small, so heartbreakingly delicate that her sensual perfection of form was somehow surprising, like the tiniest fluted turbonilla that had ever escaped the pounding of the sea. Next to her, the Gulf of Mexico seemed clumsily dangerous.

Philip shivered comically as the wind lifted her full white skirt, exposing a slim, pale and graceful thigh. "Ooo-weee, man, is she hot," he said, exhaling a liquored breath.

For one hot black instant, Mark thought he might shove his cousin, thrusting him from the window, denying him the right to watch. *Shut up*, he wanted to shout. He hated the tone, the bawdy, half-drunk lechery...

Somehow he checked himself. Philip didn't understand. How could he? He saw only the high, rounded breasts, the long blond braid...

Mark saw more, felt something completely different from Philip's lip-smacking lust. And yet lust was part of it. His fingertips pulsed with a burning awareness. He wanted suddenly, almost painfully, to touch her.

She needed to be touched—he felt it as keenly as if she had cried her need out loud.

She might have been a little girl, lost and afraid, except for the somber, self-possessed quality of her slow march toward the water. Not lost, he thought, the clamps tightening in his gut. Exiled, rather. Sent out unarmed to meet the demon.

"Goddamn it, you two voyeurs knock off that gawking and get to work." Edgerton's voice cut through the strange, tingling fantasies like a cold dousing, and Mark looked at his cousin, oddly surprised to remember that Edge was in the room.

Good God. He squeezed his eyes, trying to clear his vision. What the hell was the matter with him? He needed a new woman in his life about as much as he needed sunstroke. He must be more tired than he'd thought. Yes, that was it. The gauzy silver-blue mist was playing tricks with his tired brain.

"Somebody has to meet the temps." Edgerton was shuffling papers irritably. He flicked on the light over the bar. "And this timeline just doesn't work. I don't know who we're going to get to staff the pressroom."

Mark bit back his irreverent response. He might as well cooperate—the Moonbird Hotel's grand reopening was also designed to kick off Edgerton's campaign for a seat in the state legislature, so the poor guy was doubly uptight. He wasn't going to rest until Mark and Philip were marching in lockstep, alongside the army they'd already hired.

Mark straightened, turning away from the window, ignoring the stupid pinch that felt like the snapping of a psychic cord. Nonsense. There was no such thing.

But as he crossed the room toward his cousin, hand outstretched to accept the typed agenda, he couldn't help looking over his shoulder, just once, to convince himself that he had been seeing things.

It was merely another woman. Gorgeous admittedly, but ever since he'd turned eighteen Mark had been littering the beaches of Moonbird Key with beautiful women, lovers who had foolishly dreamed of possessing him—or perhaps his money. He had buried those dreams without regret, like so many pirated jewels smothered under the thick, wet sand.

Yes, he'd been around far too long to start spinning Andromeda fantasies about a total stranger. It had to be the mist. One last look...

But, God help him, the one last look was fatal. While he watched, the woman bowed her head and, as if someone had cut the strings that had been holding her erect, suddenly crumpled to her knees at the water's edge.

He could hardly bear to watch. She was, somehow, the personification of pain. Incoming waves frothed around her legs, lifting her sodden white skirt, then sucking it down into the sand, but she was oblivious. She lowered her face into her hands, and her shoulders began to shake softly, as if her heart was breaking.

Mark made a low noise in his throat and, without a word, strode past Edgerton, who stood frozen in disbelief, his hand full of typed agendas thrusting at empty air.

"Hold on there, buddy. Where do you think you're going?" His words were aimed at Mark's back like buckshot. "After that girl out there? For Pete's sake, man, you don't even know who she is! You don't even know if she's a paying guest."

Mark hadn't intended to stop, hadn't meant to respond, but he found himself pausing once again in the doorway. What an officious hypocrite the man was! The only thing Edgerton liked better than a pretty blonde was a pretty blonde with money. Twenty years of repressed anger surged to the fore, temporarily subduing twenty years of kinship.

"You may find this hard to believe," he said as calmly as he could, though his hands had folded into involuntary fists, "but I really don't give a damn."

Glenna McBride hardly knew why she had arrived at the Moonbird Hotel so early. She wasn't due for another four hours—and Purcell Jennings, the photographer she would assist on this assignment, wouldn't arrive until dinnertime tonight.

So why was she here now, prowling this empty, seaweed-strewn beach in the half-light of dawn? Wasn't this gesture a little too melodramatic for a woman who prided herself on her practicality and emotional control?

Morbid, that's what it was. And she did not do morbid—except perhaps in her dreams.

She should at least have brought her camera. This haunted landscape would make wonderful pictures—especially *her* kind of pictures. Purcell Jennings might be the acknowledged king of lush, colorful coffeetable books, but Glenna was getting fairly good with black-and-white film.

She checked her watch, making an automatic note of the time. Five forty-five. Dawn was only a pearly promise on the horizon. The water was gunmetal gray, and the shore was a ribbon of silver, dotted blackly with bits and pieces of seaweed, shells and driftwood. Playthings of the sea gods, dropped carelessly like toys at bedtime when the tide receded.

But what difference did it make what time it was? She wasn't going to return some other morning to take photographs no matter how interesting the lines and shapes of this monochromatic landscape.

She hated the Gulf of Mexico. She had no desire to capture its undulating malevolence and hang it on the living-room walls.

Look at it now... Like a patiently crouched jungle beast, it hardly moved, the rhythmic breathing of the tide its only sound. Its surface was calm, giving no hint of the strange creatures that peopled its depths or the blind currents that blew across its floor, stronger than any human could imagine—or withstand.

But she knew. God help her, she knew.

Glenna shivered though it was not cold. Try as she might, she couldn't rid herself of the fantasy that the water was waiting for *her.* It was as if, in her long years of hating it, she had made herself its enemy. Now it recognized her, and it was deciding what to do with her.

"Hogwash." Embarrassed by her lapse into melodrama, she spoke aloud. She had always rather liked that word, which was used frequently by the son of her neighbors back in Fort Myers. She had heard him say it to his boastful friends and had admired the succinct but encompassing disdain it conveyed. "Hogwash," she repeated, but it didn't have the same authority out here in the strange, misty dawn. She shivered again.

She'd been standing too long in one place and she felt the soggy sand give slightly under her heels. She pulled her sandals off and held them behind her back, but that didn't help much. The ooze of the sand between her toes was disturbing, too, and she had to will her legs to start walking.

If she kept going, she thought, she would soon walk right into the Gulf. Would the water recognize her? Would it associate her with Cindy? Or would it even remember Cindy? Had it perhaps swallowed her so greedily it hadn't taken time to know her?

A bird burst suddenly from the mangrove trees just behind the hotel, its wings beating the air noisily. Her heart beat, too, with great, swollen thumps, and she had to fight the urge to run back toward the hotel. She'd been running for ten years, damn it. It was time to face the enemy.

Somehow she held her ground. But what, she asked her stabbing heartbeat, had she hoped to accomplish here, at this ungodly hour, ten years after Cindy's death?

Had she thought the ocean would speak to her, giving up its secrets?

Was she trying to vanquish her nightmares by reliving them? Did she really expect to see Cindy floating here now, her blond hair matted with seaweed, her blue eyes wide with dead horror, the way she floated through Glenna's dreams?

Cindy...

Touching her face, she realized that salty tears were running down her cheeks, dropping to endless anonymity in the sodden sand. She looked at her damp fingertips, confused. She had never cried over Cindy, not even ten years ago, when as a scared twelve-year-old kid she had been told that her glamorous, golden sister was dead.

But maybe, she thought in numbed surprise, that was what she had come for. To cry. To let go.

Surrendering with a strange sense of relief, Glenna fell to the sand, lowering her face to her hands. She doubled over tightly, almost unaware of the small shells that dug into her forearms. *Cindy*...

And then suddenly she was sobbing openly, harsh, desperate sounds that rang through the misty air. It was as if ten years of tears had been magically preserved, waiting for this day.

She wept for Cindy, who had been so willful. If only she hadn't been so determined to snare one of the wild and sexy Connelly boys. The boys flirted carelessly with all their pretty guests. But only one of them had died.

She wept for herself, too, for the loneliness and the guilt she'd held inside so long. If only she had called out the moment she saw that darkly tanned male hand reaching in through the window, balancing Cindy as she climbed over the sill.

"I'm awake," she should have cried. "Don't go."

She buried her face deeper into her hands, trying to shut out the visions. Her sister's blond hair in the moonlight, the man's hand....

On the inside of the wrist was a small tattoo, just two inches long but unforgettable. The moonlight gleamed on the design, and Glenna had recognized it instantly—the legendary moonbird, its outstretched wings undulating eerily.

The moonbird. Only three people wore the moonbird tattoo—Edgerton, Philip and Mark Connelly.

For years, the bird had flown through her dreams every night. Strange and ghost white, silent and menacing, its wings pumping up and down slowly, beating with some primitive rhythm that was both sensual and dangerous. Oh, God, *Cindy*... If only they had both been a little older, a little wiser.

The flood of tears had finally begun to slow. She rested her forehead on her knees, not caring that her hair was mopping the muddy sand. How long had she been crying? Her chest hurt; her eyes burned. She felt as limp as a strand of seaweed. No wonder she had postponed this emotional storm for so long. It hurt. It hurt like hell.

Lost in the pain, she didn't hear the footsteps approaching. The cool hand on her back was a shock, and with a gasp she lifted her head, peering with swollen eyes into the glimmering dawn light.

A man knelt beside her, hovering protectively, the way he might have bent over a wounded bird. His faint scent of clean masculinity mingled with the musky smell of the mist. He smiled, just a little.

"You know," he murmured softly, skimming his fingers lightly across her shoulder blades, "an old Indian legend says that the ocean was created from tears. And all mankind will have to share in the making of it."

She blinked at him, bewildered, half-mesmerized by the gentle touch, the unexpected words. His voice was low, sensual—but somehow casual, as if he was merely continuing a conversation they had begun a long time ago. As if he was completely comfortable with both legends and tears.

"But surely," he went on, drawing aside a strand of hair that had stuck to her forehead, tucking it behind her ear, "no one heart should have to contribute so many."

She didn't speak. She couldn't. His eyes were impossibly green, she noticed irrelevantly, fringed with the blackest lashes she had ever seen. And his hands were strong. Masculine. Deeply tanned. Hands that women dreamed about...

Her gaze fell slowly to the inside of his wrist. His white shirtsleeves had been rolled back almost to the elbow. She knew what she would see. She had known ever since she had heard the first mellow syllable of his hypnotic voice.

And there it was. Like fear made visible, like the mark of Cain. The outstretched wings of the moonbird tattoo.

# CHAPTER TWO

*No*! SHE WANTED to cry the word aloud, cursing the fate that had brought him out here. *Not Mark Connelly. No...*

She couldn't be so unlucky. She'd known she would see him eventually, of course—but she had expected to meet him in an office, with Purcell Jennings at her side making the introductions. Not here, not when she was speckled with sand and swollen with tears. Not wet and defenseless and emotionally spent.

She clambered to her feet, brushing at her skirt, miserably aware that the soaked fabric clung to her bare legs. It was hopeless. She peeled one last patch from her wet thigh and then gave up.

"You're right," she said. Horrified to hear the catch in her voice, she cleared her throat and tried again. "I've cried far too much. I'm fine now."

He was still down on one knee and he tilted his head to look up at her. *Mark Connelly.*

For a moment, in spite of the tattoo, she couldn't quite believe it was true. She had remembered him so differently. Surely his full, hard lips used to have a sneering twist. And his eyes...they used to be cold, slightly cruel. Didn't they?

Ten years... Suddenly she felt unsure of herself. Just how much *did* she remember, really? It had been such a long time. That slightly saturnine arch to his black brow—she remembered that. And his intensely masculine, sexually charged aura—yes, she remembered that, too.

But somehow she had forgotten just how plain all-American handsome he was. The rising sun, which had finally burned through the mist, lit the sea green of his eyes. It touched the bronze plane of his cheekbone with peach highlights and buried itself in the healthy blue-black sheen of his thick hair.

He was hardly the decadent devil she remembered. He was actually quite beautiful.

"Really, I mean it. I'm fine now," she stumbled on, aware that she was staring. "You're right. I was just being foolish."

"I didn't say anything of the sort," he said calmly, still not rising. "There's nothing foolish about a broken heart."

She frowned. *A what?*

"My heart isn't bro—" she began, but suddenly she stopped. He knew, she realized with a horrible sensation of emotional nudity. He knew all about the pain that had been fracturing her heart into jagged little pieces.

She looked away quickly, out toward the water. The sun, climbing fast, was transforming this landscape right before her eyes.

Her stark, broody study of gray on gray was disappearing. Now this beach was Purcell's province—the Gulf a shimmering blue ribbon flung out beneath a pink-and-gold streaked sky. Blue and cream and peach-colored bits of shells were scattered along the sand like confetti.

The vivid beauty unsettled her. It was almost too perfect—like this man. Mark Connelly, her number one suspect. Had he always been so gorgeous? How could her memories have been so wrong?

She concentrated on squeezing the water out of the tip of her braid and then tried to brush away the tear trails that crisscrossed her face. But her sandy fingers deposited their gritty residue on her cheeks. She was just making things worse.

"I don't know what came over me," she said stupidly, unable to find even a sliver of her usual poise. She desperately wanted him to stop looking at her like that. "I don't usually do this…this kind of thing."

"Don't you?" Finally he rose beside her, and she took an involuntary step away. He was so tall, so male…and, even worse, so *knowing*. It made breathing difficult. "Maybe you should."

She frowned. "No—I mean…" She tried to smooth back the tendrils of hair that had escaped the tight braid and now curled damply against her forehead. "I don't need to. I'm usually much more…controlled."

"Ahhh…" He raised his brows. "Is there so much to control, then?"

She stared at him, unnerved equally by his astute perceptions and his indifference to the universal rules governing small talk between strangers. Had he always been like this? *Yes*… A sudden memory flashed through her brain like heat lightning. This same man, that same tone…

Ten years ago. Mark Connelly had been only nineteen, but he had already possessed a man's body and a lethal sexuality that even a twelve-year-old could sense.

Cindy had talked about Mark more often than any of the others. "He's not the prettiest," she'd say, "but he's the most dangerous." And when Glenna had asked why on earth anyone would want a dangerous man, Cindy had just laughed.

One day, tired of feeling invisible to the teenagers who noticed her only when they wanted her to fetch something, Glenna had wandered away to pout. She had been busy gouging resentful runnels into the sand with a seashell when Mark had plopped down beside her.

She remembered being stunned by the attention. He had been kind in a rather offhand way. Without ever actually saying so, he had hinted that he understood how rotten it was to be the youngest, to be teased and ignored and exploited. And when he had risen again after only a few minutes, he'd looked down at her with something she interpreted as pity.

"It will happen, you know," he'd said.

She had scowled, instinctively resenting any sympathy. "What will?"

"You'll grow up." He'd smiled. "And boys will think you're pretty."

She'd been too shocked to answer, staring at him as if he had just whisked a rabbit out of a hat. Without another word, he had ambled away, returning to the cluster of young men who daily attached themselves to Cindy like so many barnacles.

Back then, Glenna had been too naive to realize that it was just a parlor trick. Mark could dip into a little pop psychology, a superficial understanding of human nature, and the girls believed that he had read their minds. Other boys pretended to pull pennies out of the girls' ears—Mark Connelly pretended to pull secrets from their hearts. Same game, different props.

But now, at twenty-two, she saw through him all too clearly. He played the flirtation game even better today, and she had dealt him the perfect card. *You meet vulnerable woman weeping on the beach. Advance three spaces. Skip past small talk, enter premature intimacy.*

But he had the wrong sister this time.

"I appreciate your concern," she said crisply, "but honestly I'm fine. Actually I'd better be getting back to my car." She brushed her palms together briskly, removing as much of the sand as possible, and held out her right hand. "Thanks again."

He narrowed his eyes as if her attitude, or perhaps her tone, somehow sparked his curiosity. Taking her hand, he cocked his head and let his gaze slowly rake her face. "You seem so familiar." He lifted one corner of his lips. "This is an old one, but I have this feeling... Have we met before?"

Not a very imaginative line, but she knew that, for once, it was spoken sincerely. She felt her heart do a two-step and fought to keep her face neutral. She had always known this would be the trickiest part of coming back.

"My name is Glenna McBride," she said politely. She wouldn't lie outright—but she could pray that he didn't remember her real name. Why should he? The teenagers had always simply called her Mouse, Cindy's pet name for her tiny, timid little sister. "Hey, Mouse, here's a dollar. Go buy me a Coke, would you? And hurry—I'm dying in this heat."

Her last name was different now, too. Her parents' marriage hadn't survived the trauma of Cindy's death—they had divorced within two years. Both remarried quickly, as if eager to make fresh starts. Keg McBride, her mother's new husband, was a good man and he had adopted Glenna right away.

Mark was shaking his head. "Glenna McBride," he repeated, the name soft on his lips. "No, I guess I'm imagining things."

He hadn't let go of her hand. Glenna shifted it subtly, but he ignored the signal to release her. Glenna suspected that Mark Connelly ignored a lot of the signposts in his life.

"Did you say your car? You aren't leaving, are you? I had hoped you were staying at the Moonbird."

She took a deep breath. He didn't recognize her name. First hurdle cleared.

"Well, I am, actually," she said, plunging ahead. "I'll be working with Purcell Jennings. The photographer. He's going to take some pictures of the hotel for a book on old Florida inns."

*Slow down...no babbling, for heaven's sake.* As a member of the Connelly family, Mark would already know about Purcell.

But she plowed on, her confidence growing with every coherent sentence she managed to produce. "Purcell arrives tonight, but I came early to scout around a bit. He's not as mobile as he once was and he likes me to narrow down the locations for him first."

Yes, that was better. The half lie sounded fully authentic. She was finding her stride, regaining control.

"But that's perfect," he said, obviously pleased, as if complimenting fate for doing such a good job arranging things to his satisfaction. "I'll show you around."

Irked, she removed her hand from his with one firm tug. He looked slightly surprised—as if few women ever struggled to make their way *out* of his grasp.

Well, good, she thought, lifting her chin. An ego

like that could use a couple of knocks. And he might as well learn right now that the drooping damsel he'd found weeping on the shore was not the *real* Glenna McBride.

"I'm sorry, but that won't be possible. I concentrate better if I'm alone."

His mouth quirked. He was clearly prepared either to speak or to grin, but she didn't have time to discover which. Just behind his shoulder, she saw movement along the beach, and a strong voice carried toward them on the clear morning air.

"Mark!" The tones were deep, authoritative. With a jolt of recognition, Glenna knew immediately that the voice belonged to Edgerton Connelly. The oldest Connelly boy, the leader of the pack. Self-important, slightly bossy. How perfect, she had thought when she heard he was running for the legislature. "Mark," he said now, "I've been waiting for you."

"Edge." Mark turned toward his cousin, who looked impressively elegant but completely out of place here on the beach in his expensive suit. "I'm glad you're here. I'd like you to meet Glenna McBride."

Edgerton flashed a smile toward her, a good politician's smile that warned her he was much too busy to chat but at the same time suggested that he was awfully sorry about it. He also diplomatically refrained from noticing her disheveled state. Apparently even wet, sandy beach-weepers had been known to vote.

"Ms. McBride," he said with a smooth nod of his well-coiffed blond head. "I'm sorry to have to pull my cousin away, but he's needed rather urgently up at the hotel." He angled toward Mark. "The senator's wife will be here soon, old buddy, and you know she'll be crushed if you're not there to meet her.''

Glenna couldn't see Edgerton's face, but she thought she heard real irritation lurking under his nicely oiled tones. What the hell, the tone asked, was Mark doing wasting time with a nobody on the beach when The Senator's Wife was waiting?

*Snob,* she thought, addressing his Armani jacket.

But Mark either didn't notice his cousin's anger or didn't care. ''Sorry, Edge,'' he said cheerfully. ''Tell Philip to cut the biggest scarlet hibiscus he can find, stick it in a pitcher of sangria and take it to her room. Believe me, in half an hour she won't even notice I'm not there.''

The Armani jacket stiffened. ''Not there?''

Mark patted his shoulder. ''Sorry. I can't. You see, I had just offered Glenna my services as a tour guide.''

Edgerton made a small choking sound, but Glenna broke in quickly. ''And I,'' she said, ''had just refused them. I appreciate the offer, Mr. Connelly, but as I said, I work best alone.'' She met Mark's quizzical gaze steadily. ''Besides, I wouldn't dream of letting you disappoint—'' she lowered her tone ''—The Senator's Wife.''

Surprisingly he didn't try to persuade her. He didn't even look disappointed. Instead, he looked curious. He lifted one black brow. ''Did you say Mr. Connelly?''

''Mark,'' she amended indifferently. If he wanted to rush to a first-name basis, she could handle that. She brushed at her skirt one last time. ''Well, it was nice to have met you both—''

''But you didn't.''

She looked up, perplexed. ''Didn't what?''

"Meet me." He was studying her hard. "And yet you already knew my name."

She kicked herself mentally, realizing how close she had come to giving herself away. What a stupid move! Honestly, she must have cried her brains right out into the sand.

"Well, after all, there's no need for false modesty," she said, forcing herself to smile. "Everyone who lives on Moonbird Key knows the Connellys."

"But you *don't*. Live on Moonbird Key, I mean. Believe me, I'm sure of that." He held out his hands, palms up. "And, false modesty aside, I don't flatter myself that my fame extends much beyond the bridge to Fort Myers."

"Perhaps," she countered, wondering whether her voice sounded acerbic or flirtatious, "you underestimate yourself."

Edgerton snorted. "Oh, yeah, sure. Mark underestimates himself. That'll be the day. Well, come on, we'd better get going." His voice was more openly irritable now. He took two testy paces toward the hotel and, sensing that no one was following, turned back. "Mark. Ms. McBride said she works alone. We'd better let her get to it."

Mark didn't answer him. He hadn't taken his gaze off Glenna. She met his appraisal as serenely as possible, but the intensity in his eyes made her skin tingle. His curiosity was as tangible as a touch.

"Damn it, Mark. Mark?" Edgerton's impatient bluster was dissipating, replaced by a thin tremor of anxiety. "Mark, you know I really need you. Please?"

*Please?* Glenna's gaze shot toward the older man. Since when did Edgerton Connelly, undisputed leader of the Moonbird boys, have to say please to Mark?

Mark was the poor cousin, the one who lived at the Moonbird on sufferance, the one who hadn't a penny to his name. "Is that what makes him dangerous?" Glenna had asked her sister. And Cindy had chuckled melodically. "Sort of, Mouse," she'd said, ruffling Glenna's hair. "Sort of."

For a minute she thought Mark might ignore the desperation in Edgerton's voice. But finally she felt his gaze shift, releasing her like a butterfly unpinned, and he pivoted toward his cousin.

"You're right, Edge," he said agreeably. "We wouldn't want to intrude. Well, goodbye, then—and good scouting." He started to move away but immediately halted, as if something had just occurred to him. "You'll be at tonight's dinner dance, though, won't you? Purcell will want to come. So I'm sure we'll see each other there."

His smile was wicked. He recognized her reluctance to let him come any closer, that smile said. But it also said that he wasn't so easily thwarted. He was intrigued by her—he wanted more, and he intended to get it sooner or later. That was no surprise.

What *did* shock her was the small thrill of anticipation that shimmered through her like a silver fish skimming just below the surface of her mind. *Dangerous*, she thought with an internal shiver. Cindy had been right. This man was damned dangerous.

"Oh, yes," she said, meeting his laughing eyes, accepting and answering the challenge. "I'm sure I'll have no trouble finding you. You'll be the one dancing with The Senator's Wife, right? The one with the hibiscus between his teeth."

Actually it was much easier than that.

Even without a hibiscus, Mark Connelly stood out.

Suntanned and swarthy as a pirate in his elegant white tails, he was quite simply the sexiest man in the room.

Which was no small feat, because by nine o'clock that night the Moonlight Ballroom was awash with beautiful people. Every adult in Florida who had any pretensions to glamour, power or wealth was here. To miss the grand reopening of the Moonbird Hotel apparently was to declare oneself a nonentity.

Glenna sat quietly at a table with Purcell Jennings. Comfortable together, they didn't speak. His intense silence told her that his photographer's eye was already framing, lighting, capturing the essence of the scene before him.

And what a scene it was! In honor of the legendary moonbird, the ballroom had been renovated entirely in shades of white. The walls were covered with cream-on-ecru flocked paper; the white ash planks of the dance floor were polished to a starry gloss. A luxurious bouquet of miniature Snow Bride roses adorned each table, and overhead huge chandeliers dripped hundreds of crystal teardrops.

The invitations had requested that the guests wear white, too, and as the women swirled by, Glenna could see how the Moonlight Ballroom got its name. The shades of ivory, cream, vanilla and pearl were like moonbeams dancing on silvered water.

Glenna was impressed—in fact, she had to make an effort not to be downright enchanted. Connelly money had managed to re-create a level of splendor that hadn't been seen for nearly a century. There must be, she thought, a *lot* of Connelly money.

"You should be dancing."

Glenna turned toward Purcell, surprised. As his Parkinson's progressed, it was getting harder for him to talk, and ordinarily he confined himself to articulating only the essentials. *Film, please.* Or *Less light.* Surely he didn't intend to waste his breath trying to persuade her to dance. He knew it was futile.

"Should I? Why?" She put her hand over his, aware of how little padding covered his long, elegant bones. "I'm enjoying myself here with you. And I suspect that all this pageantry is more beautiful viewed from the outside anyway."

Purcell shook his head. "Not more beautiful," he said slowly. "Safer. You always think outside is... safer."

"Nonsense." She felt herself flushing. One drawback to Purcell's condition was that he didn't waste any time beating around the bush. He stared at her with a piercing gray gaze that shamed her. "Well, maybe," she modified, pleating the corner of her napkin pointlessly. "But what's wrong with keeping a cautious distance? What you call cowardice seems like common sense to me."

Purcell's thick white eyebrows drew together. "Bah!" His hand twitched irritably, but he didn't take it away. "Pure twaddle. You need to get to know these people if we're going to get any decent pictures. *Feel,* Glenna. Feel what this family, this hotel, are all about."

"I know, I know." Glenna smiled, trying not to notice the twinge of conscience that stung her. Purcell approached all his shoots that way—feeling the atmosphere first, then trying to capture it on film.

And for once his dictates dovetailed with her own private agenda. She *wanted* to get to know the Connellys, maybe even ask a few subtle questions.

Perhaps, before the photos were finished and their bags were packed, she might even learn which of the three young men had lured Cindy out on that fateful night.

She'd already met Philip here tonight. He might be a good place to start. He had always been the sweetest Connelly, somehow less intimidating than Mark's roguish audacity or Edgerton's handsome grandeur. Tonight he seemed to be hitting the champagne bar pretty hard. Even better, she thought. Champagne loosened tongues quite nicely.

"You know," she said, hoping to distract Purcell, "we really should have brought our equipment. You could have taken some wonderful photographs here tonight."

Purcell studied the room. "Too damn much white," he pronounced finally. "Only thing worth shooting is the food."

Glenna's gaze shifted to the huge buffet table that dominated one corner of the large room. He was right. The rich red of the strawberry pyramid, the golden brown of the stuffed Cornish hens, the bursting suns of tangerine tarts and orange scones... It made such dramatic visual contrasts with all the elegant moonbeam people.

That woman, for instance, with her multilayered choker of pearls and her elaborately coiffed blond curls, was dangling a blood red strawberry between two fingers, pressing it laughingly against the lips of a man who...

Who looked like...

Who *was* Mark Connelly. Glenna's stomach tightened as Mark slowly parted his lips and closed his teeth over the berry. Pale pink juices trickled down the woman's fingers.

With another coy laugh, she held them up for
Mark's inspection, obviously inviting him to lick them
clean. Glenna made a low, reproachful sound—this
woman, though beautifully groomed, was clearly old
enough to be his mother. *Lick* her fingers? Surely not.

Smiling comfortably, Mark circled the woman's
wrist with his thumb and forefinger and lowered it.
With his other hand, he whisked a handkerchief from
his pocket and gently swabbed at the wet fingers. The
woman pursed her lips in a mock pout, but she didn't
look terribly disappointed. She looked besotted.

Glenna turned away. She grimaced at Purcell, who
had been watching the tableau, too. "Ugh," she said.
"What a display."

To her surprise, Purcell was smiling. "Why
shouldn't they flirt?" He tilted his head. "A beautiful
woman. A handsome man. Soft moon, sweet music,
flowing wine—"

"She's twice his age," Glenna broke in irritably.
"I'm not a prude, but surely a woman of fifty—"

"Sex has no age," Purcell said firmly. "And you
*are* a prude, my dear. Just a little. You work at it."

Stung, Glenna tossed her napkin on the table, leaning forward to argue the point, but at that moment a
shadow fell across her plate. She looked up, startled,
and found Mark Connelly standing just behind her
chair. He had brought his strawberry-stained friend
with him.

"Hello," he said pleasantly. "I'd begun to wonder
if you had stood us up. I'm glad you didn't. I'd like
you to meet Maggie Levenger." He smiled right into
her eyes. "The senator's wife."

The senator's wife. Of course. Glenna summoned
up polite murmurs as the introductions were made, no-

ticing with surprise that Purcell stood to welcome the
newcomer, something he rarely did anymore.

Up close, Maggie Levenger looked even older,
maybe nearer to sixty, but her eyes were bright and
intelligent, her smile generous. Her voice was brassy,
a touch too loud, but it was full of self-deprecating
humor, and Glenna suddenly regretted her earlier hasty
condemnation.

"Mr. Jennings, I know your work well. I *adore*
you." Without ceremony, Maggie deposited herself in
the chair closest to Purcell, leaving the chair by Glenna
free for Mark.

Still smiling, he raised one brow—his only ac-
knowledgment that he needed her permission to sit.
She nodded reluctantly, reminding herself that his at-
tentions fitted into her agenda nicely. *Get to know the
Connellys, maybe even ask a few subtle questions....*

But frankly, Mark didn't seem nearly as safe a place
to start as Philip would have been. She couldn't imagine being quite subtle enough to fool Mark. And besides, he was physically too...powerful. He seemed to
send out electromagnetic signals, inviting women to
dash themselves against him like ships against the
shoals.

As if unaware of all that, he settled comfortably in
the chair, draining his drink, something clear and on
the rocks. His open gaze studied her without subter-
fuge.

"I really am glad you came," he said, his tone low
and somehow intimate. "You look radiant tonight.
Like...starlight."

Toying with her fork, Glenna shot him a look of
half-cloaked cynicism. Were his genes automatically
programmed to spew compliments when greeting any

female? Besides, it was obviously a massive overstatement. In her simple, white-beaded sheath with its demure jacket, she knew that she couldn't hold a candle to the glamorous guests in their frothing laces, their clinging satins, their cascades of pearls and diamonds.

"Surely you mean moonlight." She met his gaze directly, to show him without delay that she was not in the market for a flirtation. It would take more than free-flowing flattery to get past her defenses. "After all, that's the general idea, isn't it? *Moon*light Ballroom, *moon*bird..."

He narrowed his eyes thoughtfully, treating her comment as if it had been quite serious. "No, in your case, I think the effect really is more like starlight. Just a little sharper, brighter than moonbeams, you know. A shade less mellow." He smiled. "But also a shade more exciting."

She stared at him, momentarily at a loss. "Well," she said finally, "I've washed off most of the sand since you saw me last. That's undoubtedly an improvement over this morning."

He let his gaze run slowly across her collarbone, down her arms. "I don't know about that," he said. "A dusting of sand can give a woman a rather primitive appeal, don't you think? Earthy. Abandoned. Sensual."

She shifted on her seat, wishing he didn't have such an uncanny knack for getting under her skin.

"On the contrary. It's dirty. Gritty. Uncomfortable." She punctuated her words by tapping her fork against the tablecloth. "I much prefer to be clean, brushed and pulled together."

"In control." He raised that eyebrow again, and she was struck anew by the brilliance of his green eyes.

They were more dramatic than ever in this room full of colorless moonlight, like two emeralds blazing in a bed of seed pearls. "You like control, don't you? You need it."

"Of course I do." Her voice was slightly thin. "Doesn't everyone? Don't you?"

He considered. "In its place, I suppose I do. I definitely enjoy control over my finances. And my enemies." He paused. "But I place a higher value on freedom. I've always believed that a little judiciously placed abandon makes life worth living."

Her smile felt brittle. "Judiciously placed abandon? Isn't that a contradiction in terms? Is there such a thing?"

"Of course there is," he said, leaning back. "Here's a good example. You've decided not to dance with me." He raised a hand to quiet her confused denial. "Yes, you have. I could see it in your eyes when I sat down. You froze up like the Snow Queen. And why? Perhaps because you're afraid to get that close to me. You're afraid you'd lose a little control, maybe melt that icy casing just a little."

"Good heavens." Her voice nearly trembled. "What a preposterous—"

He didn't seem to hear her. He simply lifted that devilish eyebrow a millimeter higher and kept talking. "But I have to ask myself—what would be wrong with that? It's only a dance. Even if it was the steamiest dance since Salome, when the music stopped, you probably wouldn't find yourself morally compromised, socially ruined or pregnant." Grinning, he hoisted one long, lean leg over the other. "So you see, succumbing in this case would be a perfect example of judiciously placed abandon."

She smiled reluctantly. And then, in spite of herself, she laughed.

She couldn't help it. He made it all sound so ridiculous. And, she supposed, it probably *was* ridiculous to be so determined to keep him at arm's length. He was just a man. No real threat to her, not in the long run.

She knew his type—the consummate flirt who found her reserve challenging, but who, having once conquered it, would yawn and prowl off toward his next victim.

So why did the idea of dancing with him still feel so dangerous?

"Goodness," she protested mildly, careful not to overdo it. "You make me sound rather neurotic. But believe me, I've never once, in the whole twelve hours I've known you, been afraid of you. And I'm certainly not afraid to *dance* with anyone."

His eyes glittered with something like triumph. "Wonderful," he said, taking her hand in his. "In that case…I think they're playing our song."

The clever devil. It had all been carefully staged, hadn't it? Like a complicated chess game. But her urge to laugh was fading fast. His hand was so warm over hers. She could feel the rich blood pulsing in his fingertips.

"I would love to," she said as calmly as she could. "I truly would. Except that I really must stay here with Purcell."

Mark glanced over at the photographer, who was still lost in huddled conversation with Maggie. "Must you, Snow Queen? Looks to me as if you could take a slow boat to the North Pole and be back again before he ever noticed you were gone."

Glenna glared at Purcell, willing him to look up. But, damn the man, he seemed to have forgotten she was alive. Maggie's trilling laughter wafted toward her, and she sighed, abandoning hope.

She was stuck. She would have to stand up, let Mark fold his strong, warm arms around her, rest his tanned cheek against her ear, enveloping her in the mist of sensuality he exuded. If only she really were made of ice, or snow, or brittle, glittering starlight...

"All right," she said, swallowing her nerves and smoothing her skirt. "I'll—"

But at that moment a tiny whirlwind of organdy came swirling toward them, launching itself at Mark's knees.

"Mark! Help!" The little girl's voice was desperate, and she wound her fists into his dress shirt. "Daddy says I have to go to bed after this song. He won't dance with me, but you will, won't you?"

As Mark hesitated, the little girl twisted her head, noticing Glenna.

"Oh," she said, managing a smile through her shine of tears. "Hi, Ms. McBride."

Glenna smiled back. She had met Amy, Edgerton's five-year-old daughter, earlier that afternoon out on the beach. An uninhibited, precocious child, her yellow bathing suit slipping off one shoulder, her arms poking out to accommodate puffy plastic water wings, she'd been pathetically determined to befriend "the camera lady" and had followed Glenna around for an hour.

"Tell him to dance with me, Ms. McBride. I want to dance with Mark." Amy's stubborn frown was ferocious, but somehow, to Glenna, irresistible.

Glenna smiled up at Mark, whose rueful, one-sided grin proved he knew he'd been foiled. Leaning over, she freshened Amy's crumpled white organdy bow and patted her soft blond hair. "I'm sure he would be honored, wouldn't you, Mark?" She kept her tone innocent. "In fact, he was just saying that he felt like dancing."

To his credit, Mark gave in graciously. "That's right, half-pint. I was."

Amy bounced gaily. "Awesome," she said, clapping her hands. "And then when we're finished, will you take me up to my room, Ms. McBride? Daddy can't leave the party, and Mamma's sick again—she's been sleeping since lunch."

Glenna looked into the little girl's expressive eyes—and, though she might have been imagining things, she believed she saw a deep longing behind the brassy audacity. What a life this child seemed to have! Building solitary sandcastles, bothering strangers on the beach. Sleeping alone in a hotel room. Daddy always busy fawning over his important guests. Mamma too frail to bother…

"Sure," she said impulsively, not allowing herself to wonder what the Connellys would think of such an intrusion. Mark could have stepped in, prevented her involvement simply by volunteering to take the little girl upstairs himself. But he hadn't said a word. "I'd love to."

"All *right*!" Amy threw her arms around Glenna's neck, indifferent to the crush of expensive organdy ruffles. "Now you'll both have to tell me stories. Two stories for me!"

"Both?" Glenna glanced at Mark quickly, her heart lurching in sudden nervous awareness. So *that's* what his silence was all about. "Two stories?"

"Yes." Mark rose and took Amy's hand. "Stories

from both Ms. McBride and me. I guess it's your lucky night." He cocked his eyebrow as he tossed Glenna a smile over his shoulder. "I think I'll tell her the one about the Snow Queen."

# CHAPTER THREE

AN HOUR later, Amy was finally asleep.

Glenna saw right away that Amy had wanted an extra bedtime companion primarily to help delay the dreaded moment when she actually had to get in bed. First she'd insisted on touring Glenna through her entire collection of stuffed animals. Then she'd made a fuss worthy of a prima donna out of choosing a nightgown, soliciting Glenna's female judgment on every detail.

Even after they'd tucked her in, she'd fought hard to stay awake. Mark had to improvise his way through *The Snow Queen*, *The Snow Queen's Revenge* and *Son of Snow Queen* before the little girl finally gave in to the exhaustion she clearly felt.

As they tiptoed out, Glenna glanced around the room, aware that she had badly misjudged at least this one element of Amy's life. Edgerton hadn't selfishly transplanted his family to the Moonbird for the duration of the campaign simply to facilitate entertaining. They *lived* here, in a charming suite of rooms on the fifth floor of the hotel. The top floor, the one with the most commanding view of the Gulf. Of course.

"Oh, Mark, it's you." A quiet, thin voice came from the far side of the living room. "I didn't know you were here."

Glenna followed Mark's gaze to the spot where a

door had cracked open to reveal a pale, dark-haired woman standing hesitantly, holding the edge of the door with both hands as if unsure whether she should shut it or not.

"Hi, Dee," Mark answered cheerfully, obviously not at all surprised to see her. "We just put Amy to bed."

The woman sighed. "Thank you," she said softly. "I was sleeping." She fumbled briefly with the lace at her wrists, adjusting it, and then, holding her robe closed around her throat, finally ventured out into the room. "I just came out to get a glass of water. To take some pills."

Mark introduced them, and Glenna had to swallow a murmur of amazement. *This* was Deanna Connelly, Edgerton's wife? She searched her memory, trying to dredge up a picture of Deanna in the old days—but she realized she had never actually seen her.

Edgerton had only just become engaged to socialite Deanna Fitzwilliam that summer ten years ago. Moonbird Key was abuzz with the news. What a catch she was, even for a Connelly!

Whenever Glenna saw Edgerton nuzzling the neck of a bikinied blonde, she would ask Cindy if *that* was the fiancée. But Cindy had always said no, of course not, Mouse. Dee the Debutante wouldn't risk getting sand in her tiara.

The bowed head of the woman standing here now didn't look as if it could support the weight of a crown. After the introductions, Deanna seemed to summon up a little energy, but the effort to make small talk clearly wearied her.

Glenna once again revised her assessment of Amy's

family. Deanna wasn't just a princess complaining over a pea. She was truly frail, apparently quite sick.

After exchanging stilted pleasantries with Glenna, she looked toward Mark. "I thought you might be Edgerton," she told him, her voice low. "But that was foolish. Of course he's busy. So many people to talk to, so much to do."

Mark put his arm around her shoulder. "Oh, you know Edge," he said lightly. "He's got to be host, chef, gardener and chief dishwasher all in one. Perfectionists are like that. He's probably down there right now telling the guy with the piccolo how to hit high C."

Deanna nodded, fidgeting with the lace around her wrist. She tried to smile, but when she looked up, her eyes were red. "I know he thinks I should be there," she said, her gaze locked on Mark, "but honestly, I'm really not well enough yet. And there are so many people...."

"Edgerton understands that, Dee." Mark's voice was even more gentle than it had been as he kissed Amy good-night. "He wouldn't have wanted you to try. He just wants you to rest and get better."

"Yes," she said, obviously clutching his reassurances like a security blanket. She patted his shirtfront gratefully. "And I think I will. If you'll excuse me, I think I'd better just go back to bed now and rest."

And then, with a slight smile that hauntingly hinted at the beautiful, vibrant woman she ought to be, she was gone.

Mark stood watching the door she had shut behind her, his face expressionless. Glenna couldn't quite imagine what he was thinking. She didn't even know what she thought herself.

"She didn't get her pills," she said tentatively, just in case it was important.

"She doesn't need them." Mark's voice sounded slightly harsh.

The silence stretched on. "Perhaps I'd better go," Glenna ventured finally, when it became uncomfortable. "I'll just say good-night to Purcell and—"

"No. Wait."

It was an order from a man accustomed to giving orders. Surprised, Glenna obeyed without thinking and watched as he picked up the phone and waited for the concierge to answer.

"Easton, it's Mark," he said succinctly. "Send someone up to the suite ASAP." He glanced at the door again. "No, I don't think we need an RN, but do make sure it's a woman. I want her here until Edgerton comes up."

No argument ensued from the other end apparently, because in two seconds Mark had hung up the phone and turned to Glenna.

"Now," he said, a hint of a smile returning to his lips, "you were saying?"

Glenna hardly remembered *what* she had been going to say. She felt a little as if she had just stepped into a very strange dream where nothing looked or sounded as she expected it to. She knew ten years was a long time but...

Things certainly had changed around here. Philip's manner downstairs had stunned her. He had seemed rather sweet and simple ten years ago, perhaps the most "normal" of the three Connelly boys. When had he changed from boyish charmer to sloppy drunk?

Now this. When had Deanna Fitzwilliam faded from trophy bride to shadow wife? And even more amazingly, how had Mark Connelly made the transformation from poor relation to power broker?

He was waiting. Desperately she found her train of thought and grabbed it. "I said I probably ought to go now. You have things to do—"

"You can't leave yet," he said, but the authoritative bite was gone from his voice. In its place was the old playful tone, the teasing note of cat and mouse. "You still owe me a dance."

"I do?" He just smiled. She looked around. "Well, even if I do, I don't see how we can—"

A soft rap interrupted her, and she closed her mouth, frustrated. Mark must think she was an airhead. She felt as if she hadn't finished a single sentence in his presence tonight.

Without comment, he answered the door, ushered in a no-nonsense woman in a white uniform, exchanged a few inaudible sentences with her and then held out his hand to Glenna. "Come with me," he said, his grin back in full force. "And I'll show you how."

She resisted, but only a little, dragging ever so slightly on his hand as he strode toward the elevator, plunged them down three stories and then swept her out onto the wide second-floor veranda.

He took her acquiescence for granted. And with good reason, she had to admit, wondering at herself. Her resistance was purely token. As his pace accelerated, her feet hurried after him as if her evening slippers had come equipped with wings.

But why? What was happening to her? She had felt slightly on edge, different somehow, ever since her fit of weeping on the beach this morning. Was it possible that letting go of some of her bottled-up grief had been therapeutic—inching aside an emotional boulder that had been blocking her for years? Or was it just the primitive animal appeal of Mark himself? His personality was so vibrant, his nature so recklessly vital, that she was drawn to it and afraid of it in equal measures.

But when she had seen him standing next to that tragic, washed-out Deanna Connelly—well, somehow in that moment the balance had shifted, and Glenna had felt a sudden piercing craving for...for the life force he represented.

Across the veranda then and around the western corner of the hotel, to where a small minaret jutted out, an architectural whimsy that had clearly been included primarily to offer an appropriate nook for clandestine assignations. Open to the night air, it overhung the first-floor ballroom, and the music floated up easily, filling the tiny tower with haunting, half-heard melodies.

Glenna looked around, suddenly disconcerted. This might have been a mistake. The orchestra was playing the "Moonlight Sonata". Of course. What else?

She tried to make a joke, something lame about Mark's impeccable timing and how much he must have paid the pianist to play that song on cue, but she couldn't quite find the right words. When she reached for a sentenceful of bracing cynicism, she came up mute. So instead, buying time, she went to the edge of the tower, looked out—and felt herself tumble over the last razor edge of resistance.

"Oh, look," she said, as breathless as a debutante herself. "How beautiful it is!"

No, not even sensible Glenna McBride could resist such a night. The sky was like a dowager wearing all her jewels at once—a thousand diamond-chip stars glittering across her dark blue velvet breast.

As Glenna watched, the round moon smiled, then retreated behind a drifting veil of silver lace. And below, more beautiful than all the rest, lay the black satin Gulf, dancing a silent, erotic waltz with the wind.

"Yes, it is." Mark was right behind her. Her pulse sped slightly as he put his hands on her shoulders. "Very, very beautiful," he murmured, and turned her toward him.

Did they dance? Perhaps. But her body was registering so many rhythms at once it was difficult to know which one to follow. The heavy rolling sweep as the tide stroked the shore; the soundless, measured throb of Mark's heart against her hand; the languorous trickle of moonlight through the piano keys.

No dance she'd ever learned could encompass all of that. They moved slowly. Sometimes not at all.

"Relax." His voice was low, insistent, very near her ear. "Remember—it's only a dance."

But how could she? It was so strange to hold him like this—sweet and dangerous at the same time. Without taking a single physical liberty, he made it an act of amazing intimacy.

She stiffened her spine, which seemed to want to melt into itself. *No*. She might have surrendered to the beauty of the night, but she hadn't relinquished her soul to *him*. Yes, that was right, hold something back. She was determined to keep one part of herself untouched, one corner of her mind that the music and his scent couldn't infiltrate. *Outside is…safer*.

But it was so difficult. Her fingers trembled against his back from the effort. She felt as if she'd never really heard the sonata before—had there always been such a deep, insistent counterpoint below the softer, rippling treble notes? Where once she had heard lovely sadness, lovers parting beneath the moon, she now heard something different. They were not parting— they were coming together, and the experience was both glory and despair, death and redemption....

*It's only a dance.*

But now his firm, long fingers were tracing the contours of her spine—the muscles contracted in his wake, arcing her toward him. Her eyes drifted shut; her skin warmed where it met the ridged wall of his chest.

She felt his power slipping inside her defenses; the safe corner of her mind buckled dangerously under the pressure. He wasn't a man who tolerated locked places. He wanted it all, expected it all, whether it was for the length of a sonata or for a lifetime.

*It's only a dance.*

Somehow, by sheer will, she held on, and when the music stopped, she pulled back slowly. She looked at him, bewildered by how depleted she felt. She touched two fingers to her temple as if she could corral her thoughts. But it was like trying to force rain back into the clouds, tears back into your heart.

"That was...lovely." She tried to smile lightly. "Your orchestra is very good." She pushed a few stray hairs back into her French knot. "You know, though, I really do think I should go back downstairs now."

"Let me guess." His tone was softly mocking. "Purcell needs you?"

She laughed awkwardly. "Well, yes. Surely by now the senator has come to claim his wife—"

"I hope not. The senator died ten years ago." Mark leaned against the balustrade. The full moon rimmed his dark hair in silver. "We call Maggie the senator's wife out of habit. No, actually I suspect she probably has Purcell lounging on a chaise on the beach right now, watching the moon and drinking sangria."

"Oh." Deflated, Glenna looked out toward the Gulf, as if she might be able to spot Purcell and Maggie. "But Purcell doesn't drink."

"No?" Mark chuckled. "Well, then they won't be back for hours. If Maggie has the whole pitcher to herself, she'll be doing the dance of the seven veils for him at dawn."

Glenna tried to picture it. It was simply too preposterous. "I think," she said stiffly, "that you underestimate Purcell."

"Because I believe he's capable of keeping pace with Maggie? And still man enough to want to?" He shook his head. "No, Glenna. You're the one who does that."

Flushing, she kept her gaze trained on the beach, and finally her eyes grew accustomed to the dim light enough to pick out the dozens of couples strolling along the dark, wet sand.

Apparently, when it came to the behavior of guests at Moonbird Hotel parties, Mark knew what he was talking about. A boardwalk led across the small, grassy dunes toward the beach, and a pile of discarded evening shoes glittered at the foot of the steps. How many barefoot Cinderellas were out there right now, she wondered, ignoring the chime of midnight?

Suddenly Mark stiffened at her side, and he made a low, annoyed sound that might have been a half-expressed curse.

"What is it?" She glanced at him, but his face was under a rigid control as he stared down at the scene below. She tried to see what he saw, but she couldn't identify any of the entwined silhouettes. "What's wrong?"

But then she spotted the problem. Edgerton was coming up the boardwalk toward the hotel, obviously returning from a walk along the beach. At his side was a very young, very tipsy woman whose laughter was just loud enough to reach the tower.

It was clearly not Deanna.

"Oh," Glenna said stupidly. She waited for Mark to comment, to express his disgust, his embarrassment, that she had witnessed this. Or, perhaps, to try to gloss it over.

He didn't. He was silent, inscrutable, watching wordlessly.

"I think I know her," Glenna said suddenly, surprising herself by speaking. Was *she* going to do the glossing? How ironic. "I met her earlier tonight. She's the daughter of one of Edgerton's big contributors, someone in citrus, I think. So that's probably what he's... Well, you know how it is for politicians...they have to kiss a lot of babies, indulge a lot of bigwigs' daughters...."

Mark shot her a strange look. His eyes glittered in the moonlight, which made them seem to have a sardonic expression. "Is that what you really think is happening down there?"

"I don't know—I—"

But at that moment, Edgerton and his lady friend stopped just short of the hotel. He pulled the young woman into his arms. Though the orchestra was between songs, the two of them danced...apparently hearing the music in their own minds. Slowly. Hardly moving. Sensual.

Glenna felt a miserable burn creep across her

cheeks, spilling down her neck. She knew that dance. It was exactly like the one she and Mark had just shared. Was that how she had looked—clinging, melting, surrendering?

Oh, God... But as she watched, a familiar, more comfortable anger began to burn alongside the shame. Why should this surprise her? Apparently it was just that time of night—time for the Connelly men to stop flirting randomly, time to pick out a woman, the way they might have picked out an hors d'oeuvre from a silver tray.

Simple, really. Mark had chosen Glenna. Edgerton had chosen this nubile citrus baron's daughter. They had even found a woman for Purcell—wasn't that thoughtful?

Suddenly Edgerton stopped dancing, and with coaxing whispers, he pulled the young woman around and led her back across the boardwalk. Back to the beach.

Glenna's chest felt hot and hard. Yes, time to withdraw to a more private spot...a darkened minaret, perhaps. Or maybe, for Edgerton, it would be a lonely stretch of shore where, unseen, a man and a woman could swim, naked in the warm, black water....

The way it had been with Cindy.

And then she realized that, in spite of the seductive night sky, in spite of the mesmerizing Mark Connelly, she hadn't really changed at all. She was still the same uptight, prudish Glenna who hated predatory men like that.

Who hated, specifically, the *Connelly* men.

She turned around and forced herself to face Mark squarely. She used her contempt like a shield against his charm.

"I'm going down to get Purcell," she said tightly,

leaving no opportunity open for discussion. "Perhaps you'd better go and get your cousin before he does something foolish."

Well, hell, all women were expensive.

He ought to know. Through the years, Mark had had women who cost him his lunch money, his beer money, his sleep, his best friend and his reputation. But this was the first time he'd had one who cost him his peace of mind.

He swatted at a low-hanging frond, which unfortunately was laden with last night's rain, and said something fiercely expletive.

He was on the last quarter mile of his morning jog, and thanks to the Snow Queen, he hadn't experienced a single second of the pleasure he usually felt as he explored the natural sanctuaries of his island.

For starters, he was running too far inland—three times he'd nearly tripped on cypress knees, and twice a haughty Louisiana heron fishing in the shallows had swiveled her neck to give him the evil eye for disturbing her concentration.

But, even worse, he'd spent the entire run trying to figure out what that damned McBride woman's problem was. Something—or somebody—had put a chip the size of Lake Okeechobee on her pretty little shoulder, that much was for sure.

At first he'd thought it was just because he'd caught her crying—she obviously wasn't the type who liked to be seen *en déshabille* emotionally or otherwise.

But it had to be more than that. Sometimes, when she looked at him, she had that bitter mixture of anger and sorrow, fear and defensiveness, that he normally saw only in the faces of the women whose hopes of wedding bells he had just crushed.

He laughed out loud at the thought—sending a couple of poor egrets sprinting, rubber-legged, off through the mudflats. Yep, that was some comment on his love life, all right. Ordinarily a woman had to know him longer to dislike him as much as Glenna McBride did after only one day.

But why did he care? Maybe, though she didn't know him, she knew *of* him. Maybe she knew somebody who knew somebody who had once hoped to be able to sign Mrs. Mark Connelly to her checks. So what? He'd just ended one of those exhausting relationships. He could use a few months off. Or a few years.

If only she weren't so damned intriguing. If only he didn't catch these glimpses of something different, more vulnerable, beneath that puritan pose, like seeing the flash of a roseate spoonbill hiding in the mangroves. It was fascinating, elusive, tantalizing…

And then there was last night. Just for a minute, while they'd been dancing, she'd gone as sweet and soft as night-blooming jasmine.

*Splat.* Lost in his fevered tangle of metaphors, he had let himself run slap into a low-hanging branch, and he got a face full of wet moss. Cursing, he peeled the stringy mess off and flicked it into the palmettos. Enough of this madness. Glenna McBride could be whatever the hell she wanted to be—jasmine or spoonbill, puritan or polar bear.

What she *wasn't* going to be was *his* problem.

\*     \*     \*

"Mr. Connelly, sir, there's a man here to see you."

The secretary was new. She didn't know that no one called Mark "Mr. Connelly, sir". That kind of obsequious kowtowing was Edgerton's thrill, not his.

"Who is it?" He wasn't happy to hear he had a visitor. He'd been in the office almost two hours now, which was about his limit. If he could just endure ten more minutes to finish this list of buy orders, he could get out and breathe some real air.

"He says his name is Mr. Jennings, Mr. Connelly, sir."

"Jennings?" Mark looked up, surprised. What was Purcell Jennings doing down here, in the Moonbird offices, before breakfast? "Send him in. And for heaven's sake, call me Mark, won't you? You're a secretary, not a Victorian parlor maid."

The girl blushed, but she looked pleased. "Yes sir. I'll get him, sir."

Hopeless. Mark irritably scribbled another ticker symbol on the memo. Edgerton was hiring them younger, blonder and more useless than ever these days. Or maybe this one was Philip's acquisition. She had an inordinately high bust-to-waist ratio, which was Philip's signature body type.

"Am I disturbing you?"

Mark stood up hastily, holding out his hand. "Purcell," he said warmly. "If I'd known you wanted to see me, I could easily have come up to your room."

"Nonsense." Purcell's handshake was surprisingly firm. "You've been listening to Glenna, I suppose. She's decided I'm at death's door and too weak to blow my own nose." He smiled, and his gray eyes held a decided sparkle. "Glenna's a dear, but she's a bit of a—"

"Mother hen?"

Purcell snorted. "Prison warden is more like it." He sat down, easing his fragile body slowly into the chair. Mark noticed the stilted motions and wondered whether Glenna's concern might be at least partially warranted.

Not that it would be any less smothering for being justified, of course. She was definitely an opinionated young woman. And that was the polite term.

"Anyway," Purcell went on when he was settled, "that's why I'm here."

"Because Glenna is a prison warden?"

"Well, indirectly." Purcell waved one hand in the air. "You see, I'm planning to make a break and I need your help."

Mark smiled. "You want to borrow my hacksaw?"

"No. Something a little more time-consuming, I'm afraid. I know it's an imposition, but I was hoping you could spend some time with her over the next couple of days. Show her around, help her take a few pictures. You know. Distract her."

Light was beginning to dawn—more light, perhaps, than Purcell had intended for Mark to see. "And while I'm baby-sitting Glenna, you'll be…"

The older man grinned. "Enjoying myself with Maggie Levenger."

Mark steepled his fingers in front of his mouth, hoping to hide his own grin. "I see," he said as though considering. "Enjoying yourself by…?" Again he let his words taper to a discreet question.

Purcell's grin widened. "By doing things that Glenna would energetically disapprove of."

Mark raised one brow. "That covers a lot of ground, I'd suspect."

Purcell didn't pretend to misunderstand. "Noticed that already, did you?" He sighed. "Yes, Glenna's a delightful girl, but she does spend a bit too much time on that high horse, looking down on things."

"And people." Mark fingered the knobs of the lion's paw scallop that functioned as his paperweight. "I seem to have made it onto her must-avoid list already."

Rubbing his knuckles thoughtfully, Purcell studied Mark. "Yes," he mused. "You'd be a good deal too loose in the tie for her taste."

Mark chuckled, trying to remember the last time he'd actually worn a tie. He did have one, but he was fairly sure Philip had borrowed it about five years ago.

"Unfortunately," Purcell said with another deep sigh, "my Glenna tends to prefer the officious type. Of course, she calls it 'responsible'. You know, the type who would take his cell phone to his own wedding."

"Sorry." Mark grinned. "She doesn't like Edgerton, either."

As if mentioning his name had summoned him from the world of strangling ties and howling cell phones, Edgerton chose that moment to stick his head in the door. "Mark. Sorry to interrupt. Got that list of buys?"

Edgerton peeked into the room curiously. When he saw Purcell, he immediately shoved the door open and barged in, filling the office with expensive cologne.

Mark fought the urge to breathe through his nose. For Christ's sake, every time Edgerton bedded a new bimbo he practically bathed in the stuff. Talk about a dead giveaway. Even if Deanna were as blind as

Edgerton wanted to believe, she could *smell* what a bastard he was.

"Good morning, Mr. Jennings!" Edgerton was at his most effusive, as if he were a doctor approaching the hospital bed of a deaf patient. Mark could see Purcell practically shrinking into his chair. "How I wish I had been able to spend more time with you at the party last night! But a host never has the pleasure of settling down with his guests, does he? Still, I would have loved to hear your plans for the Moonbird book."

Mark almost choked on that one. Edge had "settled down" with a congenial guest last night all right—but Purcell wasn't ever in the running. Wrong gender. He briefly considered shutting Edgerton up by stuffing the scallop paperweight down his throat, but decided he was too fond of the scallop.

Stiffening his back, Purcell gazed up at Edgerton with a natural-born hauteur. "It's not really a *Moonbird* book, Mr. Connelly. Seven historic Florida inns will be included. And I never come to a shoot with *plans*. The inn itself will suggest my approach." He lowered his eyelids slowly. "I'm sure I don't have to tell you, Mr. Connelly, that photography is a creative art, not paint by numbers."

Edgerton looked pained to have been so misunderstood. "Well, of course not, of course not." His smile was stretched so wide it hurt to look at him. "I'm quite familiar with your work, Mr. Jennings, and I know for a fact it's genius. Pure genius. In fact, when I heard that you were going to be the one who—"

"Edge." Mark held out the list of ticker symbols. "Stock market opens in five minutes. The broker's waiting."

Edgerton resisted, but somehow they got rid of him.

Mark closed the door and, turning back toward his guest, realized that Purcell was pale, trembling slightly, clearly exhausted by the encounter. He decided to cut through the small talk, as entertaining as it had been.

"I'll be glad to dance Glenna around for a couple of days," he said, sitting on the edge of the desk where Purcell wouldn't have to speak quite as loudly to be heard. He tried to choose his words carefully. "If you're sure that's what you want."

Purcell nodded. "It is." He looked at his unsteady left hand in disgust. "I'm not a fool. I know I'm sick. But I'm just going to get sicker. If I have a heart attack and fall off Maggie Levenger's boat, so be it. I'm going to live while I can."

Mark frowned. "Don't you think Glenna would understand that? If you put it to her as plainly as you have to me?"

"No, I don't." Purcell shook his head. "Glenna doesn't take risks. She doesn't want anyone she cares about to take them, either. I could insist, I suppose. I am the boss—at least technically." He smiled wanly. "But she'd worry and hover and generally spoil the whole damn thing with her hand-wringing. No, I already warned her that I might have to rely on her more than usual this time. I promised I'd get her an assistant for any days I was too weak to work." He shrugged. "Of course, I didn't mention that it might be *you*."

Mark grimaced. "She won't exactly be thrilled."

Purcell shrugged again. "You're perfect for the job. You know things about the hotel, about its traditions and its history, that she couldn't ever discover on her own."

Mark eyed the older man quizzically. "Look, let's

be clear on this, Purcell. I'll be glad to introduce her to the hidden beauties of the Moonbird, but that's it. If you've got another, more personal agenda here, I guarantee you it's a waste of time. Glenna thinks I'm—'' He broke off. ''She really just isn't interested.''

Purcell hoisted himself carefully from the chair. ''Don't worry about her. What Glenna doesn't know about herself could fill an encyclopedia. It covers everything from A to Z.'' He put his hand on the desk to steady himself. ''The important thing is, was I wrong about *your* interest?''

''My interest? In Glenna?'' Looking into Purcell's steady, perceptive gaze, Mark had to fight the urge to dodge the question. But, damn it, he never dodged questions. It was his own personal life philosophy. Whatever it is, admit it, face it, pay for it and move on. ''No,'' he said finally. ''You weren't wrong about that.'' He shifted uncomfortably. ''So where do I look in the Encyclopedia of Ignorance? Under I for 'interested'? Or under B for 'brainless'?''

''Better file yourself under P,'' Purcell said as he moved slowly toward the door. ''For 'persistent'.''

Glenna was out on the front lawn, tightening the screw on the bottom of her tripod and squinting up at the hotel, as if imagining what her shot would look like.

She had picked a good angle, Mark could tell. From there, her camera would catch the long, two-storied veranda from the corner, showing how its gingerbread cornice wrapped all the way around the building. He had to admit the hotel looked terrific. God knew it should, after all the money Edgerton had spent on it.

It was pure Victorian fantasy. Gray shingles on the

roof, spanking white trim on all the woodwork, green-and-yellow-striped cushions on bright white wicker rockers. Tubs full of fat, overfed red geraniums. The thick green carpet of St. Augustine grass rolling down to the drive, dotted at self-consciously charming intervals by croquet wickets. The "new" Moonbird Hotel, as featured in the expensive, full-color, glossy, trifold brochure.

Mark himself had loved the old girl just as much before the renovation—when her paint was peeling and the cushions on the rockers were mix-and-match. When the grass was patchy with sandspurs, when seagulls came right up to the back porch for lunch and everything smelled of salty water and Australian pines instead of Chanel and thirty-five SPF sunscreen.

As he watched from the shadows of the veranda, Glenna frowned and moved her tripod a few inches to the right. She marched over to a Chinese fan palm and tried to fold back one of its lush, widespread fronds. She put her hands on her hips and glared at it as the frond came spilling back into place.

Mark shook his head. Glenna had more in common with Edge than he had realized. Always trying to control things that ought to be left alone—things that wouldn't thrive if you messed with them, things that possessed more natural grace than any human being could ever create.

Thank God he had forced Edgerton to establish the wildlife preserve—otherwise this whole island would be nothing more than a stage set. Forty acres of Florida as it ought to be, as it once was.

Poor, shortsighted Edge—he was so laughably easy to manipulate. He had nearly died of apoplexy at the time. *What, what, are you crazy? Do you know what those forty acres are worth?*

But Mark was the only one who could raise enough cash for the renovation, so Edgerton, swallowing so much fury his eyes bulged, set aside forty acres to remain untouched. And now that Mark had brought in a few conservation-minded backers, Edgerton had begun to brag about his "ecology-sensitive" track record during every single campaign speech.

Mark didn't even ride him about it anymore. He just let him keep bragging. With every speech, Edge became more publicly committed. He had become the conservation candidate, and now, if he was elected, he'd have to live up to the name.

Shoving out of the shadows, Mark ambled across the lawn, waiting for Glenna to notice him. He was close enough to touch her before she realized he was there. But he *didn't* touch her. That P was for "persistent"—not "psychotic".

"Nice shot," he observed politely.

She looked up, and either she actually blushed at the sight of him or the sun had already begun to burn her fair skin.

"Thanks," she said. "Purcell will probably want to change it, though."

He put his hands in his pockets. "Will he? Why?"

"Oh, I don't know." As if to avoid looking at him, she bent to peer through the lens. If only she had realized what a damn good view of her perfectly shaped rear she had just offered him, he was certain she would have knocked the camera over in her haste to straighten up again.

Looking sexy obviously was *not* on her agenda this morning. Her khaki pants were completely unwrinkled, as if she had starched and ironed the crease in them. Her white Keds and her white sport shirt were pristine, her braid tight and glossy, tied off with a clean white ribbon.

All carefully colorless, all brand-new, all stiff and unyielding.

Cosmically uptight. He felt an almost overwhelming urge to reach out and untie her braid, yank the neatly tucked shirttail out of her belted waistband, rub a little grubby earth on her knees. How the hell did she think she could capture real life, real emotion—the real Moonbird—on film if she refused to let it touch her?

Suddenly he wanted to shake the hand of the wise Mr. Jennings. Mark was going to see to it that Glenna got good and dirty today, and he suspected that he had the canny old man's blessing for the venture.

"I just know I've probably missed a better shot." Glenna finally stood erect again and put one fingertip in her mouth, as if to nibble on the clean, white half-moon nail. Realizing her mistake, she whisked it out and licked her lips nervously. She still hadn't looked Mark in the eye once. "You see, I'm always looking for line and texture because I usually work with black-and-white film. But he's looking for color, mood, romance, glamour. I can't ever see that stuff." She laughed self-consciously, as if she'd said more than she meant to. "Well, that's why he's famous, I guess. That's why he's the boss and I'm the assistant."

Here was his opening. Mark realized with surprise that he was looking forward to dropping this bombshell into her exquisitely controlled morning.

Was he becoming slightly sadistic? No, he thought, just intensely curious about this beautiful woman who had no clue how sensual she really was. Curious to see what she'd do when she heard the news—she was going to *have* to learn how to feel the mood, the romance, the glamour.

And Mark was going to be her teacher.

# CHAPTER FOUR

GLENNA shoved an exposed roll of film into her breast pocket so roughly she felt a stitch tear. Then she bit the plastic lid from the fresh container so hard she left teeth marks in it.

All in all, she admitted, she wasn't handling this very well. Two hours after discovering that Purcell had saddled her with Mark Connelly, she was still so angry she could barely see to focus the camera.

She'd spent the first hour up in Purcell's room, first assuring herself that he was all right, then arguing desperately against this insane plan. She could take the pictures all alone; she could take the pictures next week; she could hire a more appropriate assistant; she could do anything, *anything*, rather than work alongside Mark Connelly.

Purcell had merely yawned.

But why *Mark*? she had demanded, frustrated past diplomacy. What did he know about photography anyhow?

Nothing, Purcell had conceded. But he knew everything about the Moonbird, every intriguing anecdote, every secret the grand old lady was hiding in every romantic nook and cranny. They were lucky he was willing to share what he knew.

Purcell, tucked up in his hotel bed with his book of poetry open on his lap and his glasses riding the tip of his long, elegant nose, had been implacable. He wanted to rest, he said. If she really wanted to make him feel better, she'd just head on out and bring him back some spectacular pictures.

Perhaps that had been the most difficult moment of all—when she had realized that she wasn't sure she *could* take pictures good enough to please Purcell.

How horrible it would be if she failed. And if she failed in front of Mark Connelly...

Which she might if she didn't shake off this paralyzing resentment. She'd run off ten rolls of film so far and knew in her gut that every frame had been wretchedly mundane. She hadn't changed lenses, hadn't played with the lighting. She had pretty much just pointed and clicked.

"Here's a nice piece," Mark was saying as they wandered through the central rotunda, beautifully decorated in shades of blue and gold and lit by a huge stained-glass dome overhead. He stopped in front of a graceful marble sculpture, the nude torso of a woman. Her head was missing. "We think it once belonged to Marie Antoinette."

Glenna was embarrassingly slow to get the joke. She just couldn't concentrate around him, damn it; she just couldn't focus. Right then, for instance, she had been distracted by the way the colors from the stained-glass dome played across his pale blue shirt, turning it alternately violet and green and ruby red.

"Oh," she said, "I get it. Marie Antoinette. Cute."

He sighed. "Well, my humor may be lousy, but I'm right about the statue. She looks wonderful in this light, don't you think?"

"Yes." Glenna turned toward the sculpture and was astonished to see that the same luxurious colors were spilling across the figure's pale marble skin. "Oh. *Yes.*"

It was weird, off balance, exotic—and shockingly sensual. A Renoir by Picasso. One breast was bathed in a warm, rosy glow; the other, untouched, gleamed virgin white. The valley of her stomach sloped cool and violet to a darkened shadow between golden thighs.

Glenna bit her lip, feeling the answering note of sensual awareness in her own body. Yes, this was Purcell's kind of picture. She had finally found one he would approve of....

But she hadn't found it. Mark had. And suddenly, staring at the sculpture, she knew. This was why Purcell had insisted that Mark be her guide. This was the only way Purcell could hope to save the assignment.

Mark *knew*. Mark *felt*. Mark *saw*. And Glenna didn't.

But she didn't *want* to know, a voice inside her cried. Why couldn't Purcell be happy with her the way she was?

She hadn't ever billed herself as an artist, had never said her visions were worthy of a Jennings, or an Adams. She was just a soldier, a worker, a relatively efficient photographer's assistant who knew her f-stops from her filters and who was happy to hand the right equipment at the right time to the right man.

"We need to wake up your inner eye," Purcell had said so often, and she had just brushed him off with a laugh. But apparently he had meant it. And Mark Connelly had been sent to do the job, a human alarm clock.

All right, then. Let it be on his head.

"I'd like to get you in the picture, too, if you're

willing," she said suddenly. It was a toss-up whether she or Mark were more surprised to hear her say it. He raised his brows, but he didn't argue.

"Where?" he asked simply.

"Over there. If you'll just stand beside the statue, facing in the same direction she is." She fumbled in her bag for her lens. She needed to make this one a close-up, bringing the two color-washed bodies into focus and letting everything around them blur to insignificance.

She was strangely excited by the idea. The torso's smooth, idealized marble skin beside Mark's indisputably human, golden-tanned and rugged profile... Two beautiful creatures—the two extremes of sensuality. Man and his dream. Purity and passion.

She took nearly a whole roll, circling the two subjects, searching for the perfect angle, the perfect light. Mark was a natural model—completely devoid of self-conscious posturing, as if he didn't much care what the camera recorded. Or, she thought, staring at him through the lens, perhaps because he knew it wasn't possible for the camera to find anything unflattering.

He really was a frighteningly attractive man.

"All done," she said after a few minutes. Now that the creative rush had passed, she felt strangely shy, as if she might have made a fool of herself. The pictures might be awful, records of her own sophomoric excitement, nothing else. She busied herself repacking the lenses and watched him out of the corner of her eye.

He roused himself casually, as if he had forgotten why he was standing there, and smiled at her. "Shall we go upstairs now?"

Her fingers slipped. The telephoto lens banged

against the wide-angle. She looked up, praying that he hadn't heard it.

"I thought I'd show you the Moonbird Suite," he said, bending over to help her readjust the equipment. He was so close she could see the way his hair curled slightly against the ridge of his ear. "It's the closest thing to a haunted room the hotel has."

"The Moonbird Suite?" She rose slowly, hugging her satchel to her chest carefully. "Your press kit didn't mention that it was haunted."

Mark shook his head, smiling. "Well, of course not. Edgerton is promoting the Moonbird as a family vacation spot, and he didn't think Mr. and Mrs. America would exactly be standing in line to bring their kids to a haunted hotel."

No. Probably not. "What's he going to think when he hears you've told me?"

Mark put his hand under her arm and nudged her toward the west corridor. "Let's take the stairs," he said, ignoring her question. "It's only on the second floor."

She followed his lead trying to get a little ahead, hoping he wouldn't feel it was necessary to take her arm again. She was ridiculously aware of him just now—probably the result of studying him so closely for the photographs. She needed a minute to find a comfortable distance.

"I mean it," she said, gesturing to her camera. "If you tell me, and I tell Purcell, and it ends up in the book…"

Mark smiled broadly as they reached the second-floor landing. "But you're probably the safest person in the world to tell," he said, leading the way toward a corner room. He pulled a key from his pocket and twisted it in the lock. "You're a no-nonsense woman. You'd never allow yourself to believe a room was haunted." He opened the door and stood back, allowing her to enter first. "Would you?"

Of course she wouldn't. She entered the room briskly, irritated that he had turned the whole thing into a personal issue, another example of her "control" problem. It was going to be a long day.

She stopped just inside the door, amazed. It was perhaps the loveliest room she'd ever seen. Lots of floor-to-ceiling windows, brimming with sunlight. All the fabrics, from drapes to pillow covers, were done in subtle violets and blues splayed against butter-cream backgrounds. She smiled. It was without question a woman's room. And it was most definitely not haunted.

"Nice," she said, aware of cultivating a particularly breezy, "no-nonsense" tone. "I'd think Edgerton could quite safely market this room to Mr. and Mrs. America." She touched the ruffled edge of the dressing table. "Especially Mrs."

As she began setting up her camera, Mark moved toward one of the windows and looked out on the Gulf beyond. The sun was sparkling off the water like a million flashbulbs going off at once.

"Yes, this suite is delightful during the day," he said agreeably. "It's only at night that people say they hear the weeping."

She crossed her arms against a ridiculous shimmer of goose bumps. "Okay, I'll bite," she said as dryly as possible. "What weeping?"

He hitched one long leg up onto the windowsill. "One winter night back in 1918, a young woman came in and asked for this suite. She was here three days, but she stayed in her room. No one ever saw her come out. Finally they began to worry. But when they went in to check on her, she was gone.''

Glenna clicked off a few shots of the sitting area, then swiveled the tripod so that the camera focused on the beautifully draped bed. Mark's face, with the sunlight behind it, was in shadows, but she could tell he was watching, waiting to see if his story got some reaction out of her. She schooled her face into a polite skepticism, which was, of course, exactly what she felt.

"Without a trace?" Glenna squinted back into the eyepiece. She brought the bed into focus.

"Well, one trace," he said. "She had left a newborn baby. A baby girl, lying peacefully in the middle of the bed, as if she had just been fed and rocked to sleep. And standing over the baby, making low-pitched cooing noises that were strangely musical—''

"Was the moonbird." Glenna suddenly felt the need to sit. She lowered herself onto the bench seat at the dressing table, her hand still on the camera. She could see her reflection in the mirror and she looked just slightly pale.

She had to give it to him—he knew how to tell a story. His voice was calm, but the lack of histrionics made the tale sound very nearly plausible. She had almost seen the moonbird in her lens....

"Right." Mark paused. "I take it you're familiar with the moonbird."

"Just from the brochures," she lied, wondering what he'd think if he knew she had dreamed about the bird every night for years. "I know that seeing it is supposed to bring you good luck. I didn't know how the legend got started.''

"Well, now you do. Our famous namesake began her career as a nanny."

She fiddled with the aperture, though she couldn't think clearly enough to decide where to set it. She took several pictures at random. "So...who weeps?"

"The baby." Mark's voice from the shadows was still matter-of-fact. "The people who hear it say an infant cries. And then they hear the sound of a bird. Some say it's like a dove, others say it's more melodic, like a canary. And then the crying stops."

"But you don't believe that," she said, hoping she was right. She pulled out the roll of film. Another wasted roll. Purcell was going to fire her. "What do you think it really is? Bad pipes? Drafty windows?"

"No." He moved away from the window, and she could see that his face was tender, as if the story still had the power to move him. "I think that we're all of us a little lost, a little abandoned—one way or another." He moved slowly through the room, touching this and that, but always making his way closer to where she sat. "And so, in spite of how much the idea scares us, we want to believe that there are magical beings watching us, guarding us from harm, comforting us when we weep."

Glenna swallowed a sudden burning lump in her throat. "In other words, overactive imaginations."

He stopped just a few inches away from the dressing table. "Yes," he said, but he sounded disappointed in her. "It can be reduced to that, if you like."

"Well," she said, realizing that if she didn't change the subject quickly, he was going to have her in tears. She couldn't fall apart now—the opportunity to bring this conversation around to Cindy's death was just too perfect to pass up. "That's quite a story." She began unscrewing her camera, folding up the tripod, avoiding direct eye contact. "But I suppose an old hotel like this has a lot of strange stories. Over the years, the Moonbird must have seen its share of tragedy."

"Tragedy?" He appeared to consider. "Actually, most of our stories are fairly upbeat—the moonbird legend draws people who are actively hunting for happiness. And they are, of course, the people most likely to find it."

Was that a dig at her? She decided not to hear it. "Still…almost a hundred years of visitors…" How hard could she push without sounding suspicious? "Don't all hotels have those stories? You know, poker games that led to duels at dawn, star-crossed lovers who drowned at midnight…"

She couldn't believe she was doing this. And yet, she asked herself acerbically, how had she *thought* she was going to discover anything about Cindy's death? Had she really believed that they would all sit down at dinner some night, and one of the men would say, "Oh, remember that girl I went skinny-dipping with ten years ago? The one who drowned?"

She couldn't afford to be too squeamish. She'd just have to press on, carefully but relentlessly, and hope that someone said something in an unguarded moment.

"Well, sure." The word "drowned" didn't seem to have sparked any guilty confusion in Mark anyway. He was gathering up her camera case, helping like a good assistant. "Let's see…" He smiled at her over his shoulder. "Well, back in the thirties a washed-up movie star tried to hang himself from the banyan tree. But he was saturated with alcohol and passed out before he could kick over the chair."

He held out his hand to take the lens, and, with his

sleeve rolled back as he always wore it, the tattoo was
exposed. She looked at it, confusion making a mess of
her thoughts. Was that all he could offer? An unwed
mother and a pie-eyed movie star?

What about Cindy? It hurt her throat to hold back
the questions. What about the beautiful, golden-haired
eighteen-year-old girl who came to stay at the
Moonbird Hotel and never left it alive? Was it possible
that they had *forgotten* her?

No…that wasn't possible. No one could forget
Cindy. Ten years was a long time, but not long enough
to wipe a tragedy like that out of anyone's memory.
Particularly not out of a *guilty* memory.

She put a small black check next to Mark
Connelly's name in her mind.

But she was surprised to discover how reluctant she
was to do it.

They broke for lunch around two o'clock. All the seats
on the oceanside patio were taken, but Mark took the
hostess aside and murmured some quick instructions.
Before Glenna knew what was happening, a couple of
busboys had gathered a small table and two chairs
from the main restaurant and were hauling them out
to the beach.

Glenna was horrified. Surely Mark didn't expect her
to eat out *there*? Everyone was watching the elaborate
process with unabashed curiosity. Tablecloth, place
settings, one bright yellow hibiscus in a bud vase—the
whole arrangement was quickly transported to the edge
of the shore.

Her protests were in vain. "For heaven's sake,
Mark! I would have been happy to eat at the indoor
restaurant. In my *room*, if necessary." She tried not to

think of the dozens of eyes, watching, speculating. "There is absolutely no need for all this."

"Sure there is," he answered easily, tipping the boys as they went back to their normal posts. "It'll be fun."

Fun? They might as well have been on stage. Glenna couldn't imagine eating anything while everyone stared at her like this. "But we'll be so conspicuous." She dropped her voice to a whisper. "All those people..."

"What about them?" He looked back and waved at a couple of guests he recognized. "They can drag their tables out, too, if they want. It's a big beach." He bent down and removed his deck shoes with an expert flick of his fingers. "Better take your sneakers off—they've set us up a little close to the water."

When she hesitated, he made a small tssking sound of exasperation. He knelt in the sand in front of her and took her foot in his hands. She tightened her foot, resisting.

"Come on, Snow Queen," he said, playfully shaking the heel of her shoe. "Let go. Live a little."

*I dare you.* He didn't add the words, but he might as well have. She knew she ought to be able to stand up to him, to tell him that she simply didn't *want* to eat lunch with the tide tickling over her bare feet. That these were dry-clean-only slacks, and she didn't care to have them soaked with salt water. That this fishbowl feeling would make swallowing difficult, digestion impossible.

But she couldn't say any of those things. Suddenly, with him kneeling at her feet like a modern-day prince, she heard how fussy and uptight they sounded. It was one thing to be sensible. Controlled. Mature. It was quite another thing altogether to be a prig.

Reluctantly she relaxed her ankle. "That's right," he whispered. "Be brave, my queen. You can do it." The shoe slipped off in his hands. "Victory!" he cried, his voice full of laughter, and then his eyes widened. Frozen, he stared at her foot for a long, silent moment. And then he lifted up to her a face so melodramatically dismayed that she almost laughed out loud at the sight of it.

But what was so funny—so ridiculous that he should assume that foolish tragicomic mask? She wiggled her toes. And then she remembered....

Panty hose.

"I should have known," he said, his voice hushed, as if the entire situation left him awestruck. "I really should have guessed." His smile broadened wickedly. "I don't suppose there's any hope you're the red-lace-garter type?"

She shook her head, trying not to blush. She'd never worn a garter in her life.

"Of course not," he sighed. "What was I thinking?"

"Well, good grief," she said, shamed into action. "What are you waiting for?"

Planting the nearly bare foot firmly in the sand, she held up her other foot, dangling it near his hands. "You'd think a little nylon was a suit of armor."

The look he gave her before he bent to his task was equal parts mirth and approval, and she felt absurdly pleased to have won it.

*Nonsense*, she told herself stringently. The approval of a man like Mark Connelly was the easiest thing in the world to get. *Take your shoes off? Well, he'd grin*

*ear to ear if you stripped stark naked. If you went to
bed with him, he'd probably give you a medal.*

But it did feel good, letting the chilly waves bubble
toward her toes while they sat at their waterside table
and ate salmon crepes with grapefruit sauce.

The food was divine, and Mark was at his most
debonair, telling amusing anecdotes about his early,
ignoble efforts to learn to surf. One story in particular,
which involved mistaking his best friend for a shark,
made her laugh so hard she nearly wept.

Gradually, as he no doubt intended she should,
she forgot about their audience. She concentrated instead on Mark, how appealing his lightly self-effacing
humor was and how attractive he looked out here with
the sequined ripples of the Gulf flashing golden light
onto his high cheekbones.

When she finally looked back toward the hotel, she
saw that most of the other diners had returned to their
own conversations. She and Mark had been a ten-
minute wonder, and the novelty had already worn off.

"You see?" Mark said, obviously following her
train of thought. "It doesn't really matter at all, does
it?"

"What doesn't?"

"What other people think."

Mark leaned back in his chair, stretching his long
legs out so far his bare toes touched her nylon-covered
feet. She shivered at the sudden warmth after the chill
of the wet sand, but she didn't pull away. It felt rather
nice.

"No human being is ever quite as interested in other
people as he is in himself." He smiled wryly. "So you
can always count on even the most annoying busybody

to wander off eventually, if you ignore him long enough.''

She didn't quite know how to answer that. It was probably true, and yet it sounded terribly cynical. She wondered briefly whether there might be sides to free-and-easy Mark Connelly that she hadn't discovered yet.

''Speak of the devil.'' Mark was looking over her head. ''Here he comes now.''

She twisted, wondering what he meant. Striding toward them with a look of intense exasperation came Edgerton. Philip followed close behind, looking more amused than anything else.

''Mark.'' Edgerton stood a little back from the table, far enough to protect his five-hundred-dollar shoes from the incoming fingers of chilly surf. ''Ms. Mc-Bride.''

Glenna smiled. Edgerton had been much nicer to her ever since he had learned that she was part of the photography shoot. Clearly he regretted having brushed her off on the beach the other morning. Photographers who might bring him free publicity were not to be slighted. And it hadn't hurt that she cleaned up well. He obviously gave special treatment to any reasonably attractive blonde under thirty.

Right now, though, he was hard-pressed to keep that smile on his face.

''You know, Mark, I've been trying to find you all day.'' He sounded extremely frustrated, as if Mark had been willfully elusive.

Glenna studied Edgerton's arrogant good looks and wondered what the cousins' relationship really was. She continued to be perplexed by the strange power dynamic between them.

"I've looked everywhere," Edgerton complained.

Mark grinned. "And now, it seems, your efforts are rewarded."

"Right." Edgerton glanced sourly around as if he'd like to complain about the irregularity of the luncheon, too, but he apparently thought better of it. "Well, I wanted to know why you left Miller's Landing off your buy list this morning."

Mark's brows shot up. "For the same reasons I gave you yesterday, Edge," he said pleasantly, as if he were speaking to a child. "Because the whole retail area is built too close to the water, the structure isn't sound, and the builder is a crook. I don't want any part of it."

Edgerton flushed a deep purple that clashed dreadfully with his sunny blond hair. "Well, *I* do."

Mark tilted his head. "Edge, come on." He shoved the platter of fresh fruit toward his cousin. "Relax. Have a grape."

"I'm telling you, Mark, I want to buy that property. If we don't do it by five o'clock tomorrow, we lose our chance. Damn it, you haven't even seen the place. How can you say it's not sound?"

"I know the builder, Edge. My gut's telling me to steer clear of this one."

"Well, your *gut* can just—" Edgerton broke off with an effort, glancing toward Glenna. "Your gut could be wrong, damn it."

Mark scooped up an orange wedge and, pushing his chair back, stood, stretching slowly. "Will you excuse us for a couple of minutes, Glenna? Edge needs to talk a little business."

She nodded. What else could she do? She wondered

if the situation was going to turn ugly, but she couldn't think of any way to head it off.

There couldn't be two more disparate styles, she thought as she watched the two men walk away. Edgerton was scrupulously groomed, elegant, every inch a millionaire born to lead, a politician born to rule. Mark, on the other hand, was in battered jeans that were soft-molded to his trim, powerful body. His hair was styled by the wind, and his feet were bare. But it was clear from Edgerton's angry gesticulating that Mark was completely in control of this situation.

"Well, I guess that just leaves us." Philip plopped himself into Mark's vacated chair and grabbed the grape Edgerton had refused. "Edge ought to know better than to cast aspersions on our cousin's gut," he said mildly. He was watching the argument, too, watching Edgerton grow more heated, his forefinger jabbing the air next to Mark. "Mark's got the luckiest gut on the planet. I say we should have the darn thing insured by Lloyd's of London."

Glenna couldn't help smiling. Philip was sober today, and he was much more the fresh-faced, pleasant young man she remembered. She hoped that last night's messy drinking had been an aberration.

She remembered liking Philip a lot, way back when. He was handsome, but he didn't have either the intense power of Edgerton or the coiled sexuality of Mark. He was just a very nice, normal guy. It was rather a refreshing change.

"I gather Mark makes your investment decisions," she said tentatively. She didn't know how much of this she ought to pry into.

"Oh, yeah. If it weren't for Mark, the Connellys would be an extinct species here on Moonbird Key.

Edgerton's gut gives really lousy financial advice.'' He chuckled and popped another grape. ''Had us within spitting distance of Chapter 11 about five years ago.''

*Bankruptcy*! ''I'm surprised to hear that,'' she said, amused by her own understatement. Shock was more like it. Bankruptcy was a big word. Mark had somehow brought the Connellys from that dark abyss to this gleaming prosperity. *Mark*? ''After all, Mark doesn't exactly look like your average financier, does he?''

''Aw, don't be fooled by that mellow beach-bum act. The guy's richer than we are.'' He smiled self-consciously. ''And he's made us pretty rich now, too.''

His gaze once again sought the other two men, who had finally turned around and were making their way back to the table.

''Besides, Mark's not your 'average' anything,'' Philip went on. Glenna heard a touching pride in his voice. Edgerton might chafe under his cousin's success, but Philip obviously was happy for Mark. ''He's a genius—money just *speaks* to him, you know? And I guarantee you he can walk into a boardroom full of stuffed shirts and have 'em trembling in their Bruno Magli shoes within five minutes.''

The two men were almost upon them. Mark was so close she could see the subtle ripple of muscles under his pale blue oxford button-down, the graceful, lazy shift of his tight hips inside his jeans. The stuffed shirts were lucky, she thought as she watched, hopelessly bewitched. Trembling in your shoes wasn't too bad.

Getting charmed right out of them was somehow much more dangerous.

# CHAPTER FIVE

THE first set of photographs Purcell shot at any new location was merely a dress rehearsal—a quick walk-through to suggest what might be worth coming back to later. Even for Purcell, that first set usually ended up in the trash can.

Which was why Glenna could hardly believe her luck: three of the pictures she had taken during these past two days with Mark were fairly good. They weren't perfect; they weren't even half as creative as Purcell's best. But they were *good*. She was elated.

The first was an overall view of the hotel that she had taken with a wide-angle lens. The sun had been perfect, highlighting the shimmering silver water behind the hotel. Even the palmetto frond that had so annoyed her at the time looked planned, falling gracefully in from one side, giving the picture depth.

The other two were of Mark. She hadn't realized that she had caught him in any of the Moonbird Suite shots, but there he was at the window, a pensive silhouette haloed by streams of golden light. Beside him, the blue-violet of the bed looked cool, inviting, surprisingly sensual. It was the kind of picture that seemed eager to tell you a story.

Best of all, though, was the shot of Mark standing next to the sculpture. She bit her lower lip, trying to hold back a shamefully juvenile gasp of glee. For the first time, a photograph she'd taken was every bit as exciting as she had imagined it would be. Perhaps more so. The colors were even richer than she had remembered—it was almost as if Mark himself were made of stained glass.

If Purcell hadn't left her a message saying he was asleep and didn't want to be disturbed, she probably would have taken all three photos, still damp from developing, up to his room. He'd been out of commission for two whole days now, and although she and Mark were finally beginning to work fairly comfortably together, she was worried about Purcell. It just wasn't like him to give in to his frailty.

But it was almost two in the morning, and she couldn't wake him. Instead, she forced herself to go over all the proofs, making adjustments for tomorrow. She spread them out on the table, frowning. This view of the beach was boring…maybe she should have waded out in the water a few feet. The ballroom was hopelessly overexposed. And this shot of the bar… She gnawed at a nail. Maybe she should reshoot the bar at night.

Lost in her plans, she heard the knock at her door twice before she realized what it was. Her breath tightened. Who could it be? Was Purcell all right?

She scrambled to the other side of the room, hardly remembering that she wore only a pair of short cotton boxers and a T-shirt, and fumbled with the latch.

But it wasn't Purcell. It was Mark. She stood there stupidly, wondering what to say. Suddenly the boxers and T-shirt seemed like a huge problem. She stifled the urge to use the door as a shield.

"Yes?" She wished she had rebraided her hair after

she washed it. It was tickling her shoulders in the most disagreeable way. "Is everything all right?"

At first he didn't answer. His green eyes looked gray in this light, and his gaze raked slowly down her body, all the way to her completely bare feet, before returning to her face.

She crossed her arms over her chest, realizing that the cooler air from the hallway was rushing into her room. "Is everything all right?" she repeated. "It's really very late, Mark."

"But you weren't asleep. I saw your lights." He smiled. "Have you looked out your window tonight?"

"My *window*?" She drew her brows together, confused. Of all the things he might have said... "No. Why?"

"Because the moon is full and white and unimaginably beautiful."

She wondered if he had been drinking. "Yes, well..." She tossed a perfunctory look over her shoulder. "That's nice."

"It's much better than nice," he said. "It's perfect." He checked his watch. "Or it will be in about twenty minutes. So hurry up. Throw on some clothes and let's go."

Yes, he *must* have been drinking—though she couldn't remember ever having seen Mark with liquor in his hand. But this was crazy.

"It's the middle of the night," she protested. "Where on earth do you want to go?"

"Just trust me," he said briskly. "Hurry. And bring your camera."

Her camera? "Listen, Mark, you're going to have to tell me what this is all about."

He cursed under his breath. "For God's sake,

Glenna, can't you just *go with it*? What's the problem? I'm asking you to get dressed, not undressed. I'm asking you to come out, not begging you to let me in. And I'm telling you to bring your camera. How much more innocent could a guy get?'' He put his hands on her shoulders. ''So it's two in the morning. So what? Just go get dressed.'' He grinned, plucking at the shoulder of her T-shirt. ''Or, better still, *don't* get dressed. Come as you are.''

''Don't be absurd.'' She backed away, shifting out of his grasp. ''Of course I'll get dressed.''

''Good idea,'' he said smugly, coming into the room and pulling the door closed behind him. ''But make it quick. There's no time for those god-awful stockings.''

Fifteen minutes later, in blue jeans and a sweater, her hair brushed if not braided, she found herself walking through moonlit palms toward a small cottage that adjoined the hotel. The night air was cool, quiet except for the dull, pebbled whoosh of the tide in the distance. Her camera slapped silently against her hip with each step.

''*Now* will you tell me where we're going?'' Her voice was low, but it seemed to carry on the still air.

He touched her elbow lightly, warning her of a fallen coconut, steering her around it. ''Sure,'' he said, still infuriatingly smug. ''We're going to my place.''

She felt her sneaker scrunch on the oyster-shell path as her feet lost their rhythm. But she refused to give him the satisfaction of expressing any open surprise. ''Why?'' She posed the question calmly, or at least she hoped she did. ''What's at your place?''

''The best view of the Moonbird Hotel from anywhere on this island,'' he said as they finally reached the front porch of the two-story cottage. ''And the

moon is floating right over her roof." He opened the
door and stood back, inviting her to enter first. "I
thought you'd like to see it."

There was no time to notice much about his cottage,
except that it was clean and spare and masculine. She
saw what might have been a rather shockingly expensive oil painting of the Everglades over his sofa, but
he wasn't offering a tour.

He detoured them briefly through the kitchen, where
he grabbed two glasses and a wine bottle, a loaf of
round bread and a block of cheese from the refriger-
ator. Then he pointed her toward the staircase.

"Upstairs?" She clutched her camera rather tightly
in both hands.

"Upstairs," he confirmed, nudging her from behind.
She felt the cool neck of the wine bottle pressing between her shoulder blades. "Turn right at the top, then
take the first door on the left. That's my room."

Oh, this was a colossal mistake. Even as she took
the stairs on feet that were suddenly numb, Glenna
cursed herself for a fool.

This was just about the oldest scenario for seduction
in the book, wasn't it? *Come on over to my place.
Come see the great sketches...etchings...view from my
bedroom window....*

"Okay, here we are." He pointed across the room.
"See that far window?"

They had just entered the spacious corner room. At
first Glenna couldn't see any windows. All she could
see was the double bed, its rumpled sheets unnaturally
white in the moonlight. *His* bed...

She tore her gaze away. "Yes, of course I see the
window," she said, testy.

"Good. Climb through it."

She didn't move an inch. She wasn't sure she even blinked. *Climb through it?*

He set the food and wine down with a tiny clink of glass against glass. "Here, let me help you." He led her to the window, then put his hands on her waist. "Go ahead. I'll hold you steady."

Somehow she got through it. It took her a second to find her bearings, then she simply stood there for a long moment on the gently sloped, gray-shingled expanse of Mark Connelly's roof, staring down at...

At a place that seemed to belong to another planet. At a place that belonged to fairies and enchanted birds and milky blue-white mists that might have been full of ghosts. She heard him set the wineglasses on the roof and then climb through the window after her, but she didn't turn around. She couldn't move. She was completely, hopelessly entranced.

He had timed it just right, in spite of her dawdling. The moon hung huge and low, like a mystical orb, perfectly poised over the pointed tip of the hotel's highest cupola. The lawns were covered with mist that glowed as the landscaping lights cut through it—creating the illusion that the hotel floated just above the ground. Spotlights turned royal palms into huge, white, feather-topped columns. And off in the distance, hundreds of tiny, windblown whitecaps shone like a spill of neon on the water.

"So I saw this, and I said to myself...any photographer trying to capture the essence of the Moonbird needs to be here on this roof right now." He was standing so close behind her that she could feel his breath against her neck. "Isn't that right, Glenna? No one can really say they've seen the Moonbird until they've seen her by moonlight."

She nodded as if to speak might break the spell, as if the blue-white moonlight might shatter under the pressure of her voice and fall, tinkling, to the ground.

He was right, so right. All her posing and framing today had been a charade; she'd been snapping pictures of an empty shell. *This* was the Moonbird. No one needed to prowl the dawn waiting for a flesh-and-blood bird to step out of the shadows. Here was the soaring white magic that gave birth to legends.

"Go ahead," he urged. "Get it on film."

She nodded again. Her camera felt heavy in her hands, as if her fingers were too aware, too sensitized. She *wanted* this picture. She was oddly, intensely hungry for it.

"I should have brought a tripod," she said half to herself, half to him. "Or a clamp. I'll need to expose for five…maybe ten minutes."

"I have a tripod from an old video camera." He was already reaching back through the window. "I put it here just in case."

He held it out to her, and she clasped it greedily. "Thank you," she said, her voice strangely breathless.

Did he know what he had done? He had brought her so much more than a piece of equipment. He had, somehow, over the past two days, brought her a new, thrilling passion for her chosen career. Later, when she found time for quiet reflection, she would try to understand how he had accomplished that.

"And Mark—" she touched his arm "—thank you for bringing me here, for showing me this."

"Just doing my job, ma'am." He smiled as if he understood. "I am the official photographer's assistant after all. Now forget about me. Get to work."

He sat on a flat surface between two dormer windows, his back against the corner board, one leg stretched along the roof and the other crooked comfortably up toward his chest. He broke off a piece of bread, popped it in his mouth and turned his attention to uncorking the wine bottle.

And then, though she wouldn't have thought it possible, she *did* forget about him. She forgot about everything but the camera and the picture she knew was waiting for her. She hunted for the perfect position. She even lay on her stomach at the edge of the roof, never once considering that she might fall.

She would have to bracket, just to be sure she got the right exposure—she hadn't ever taken a picture in light like this before. And which was the best spot...was it here, by the gable...or there, at the roof line?

Finally it was done. She opened the shutter and backed away carefully. Now it was time for the moonlight to work its magic on the emulsion. All she could do was wait.

"Here." As she climbed back toward the dormer, Mark held a glass out toward her. "You've earned it."

Smiling wearily, she took the cool flute and carefully lowered herself to a sitting position just to his left, where she could brace her back against the other edge of the dormer.

"To the moonbird," he said softly, extending his glass.

"To the moonbird," she echoed. "And to my clever assistant."

Mark inclined his head graciously. Their glasses clinked, and the sound purled away like a waterfall, down the shingles and over the roof, spilling onto the misty lawn below them.

They sat in companionable silence for several minutes. Glenna was happy, hugging a tiny pearl of excitement in her breast. The photograph was going to be wonderful. The hotel was just close enough to bring out the detail, yet far enough away that you could see how it dominated its surroundings. She was surprisingly confident, feeling the magic wouldn't *let* her fail.

Oh, yes. Mark had been so right....

She smiled, remembering how suspicious she'd been when he knocked on her door. How horrified when he suggested they go upstairs—like a prissy prom queen who thinks all the football players are trying to maneuver their way under her skirt.

She laughed out loud at the image. God, she *was* a prude.

Mark leaned his head back against the dormer and eyed her lazily. "What's so funny?"

She drew her knees up to her chest and propped the wineglass on top of them. "Me," she said, squinting so that the light fractured into stars through the champagne-colored liquid. "I actually thought you were bringing me here to seduce me."

"Oh?" His answering smile was wry. "Well, it's not too late. The bed's just through that window. How long have you set that timer for?"

"Only ten minutes," she answered, chuckling again. "Hardly worth the climb."

"True." He nudged her knee with his. "I'd need at least fifteen minutes just to wrestle you out of your stockings."

She wiggled her bare toes inside her shoes, conscious of a new sense of freedom, knowing it was far more than the absence of nylon. She took a sip of wine. It tasted fantastic, as cool and smoky as the mist itself.

"Besides," she added thoughtfully, "if we jiggled the camera, it would ruin my picture."

"Wow." He sounded concerned. "Your expectations may be a little high. I've been told the earth moved, but no one's ever said the roof fell in."

"Ah, well," she sighed as if that ended the discussion. "You're not ready for *me*, then."

The milky silence settled over them again. She could hear him breathing, and somewhere out there the tide breathed, too. In and out, pulled by the moon.

"I used to come up here when I was a kid," he volunteered after a few minutes. "When I was mad as hell at life, I'd climb out here and things would seem a little clearer."

She looked at him, surprised. "Did you live here as a kid, here in this cottage?" She had always thought he lived at the hotel with the others.

"Yeah," he said. "My dad died when I was about seven—and he died flat broke. My mother thought my dad's family ought to take us in. She said that I was a Connelly and I ought to grow up on Moonbird Key."

She couldn't quite read his tone. "And did they take you in?"

"Oh, of course." He tapped his wineglass against his knee. "Uncle Frank was a very generous man. A fact he never quite let you forget."

So *that* was the tone she heard. The sound of a proud spirit forced to feel beholden.

She tried to remember old Mr. Connelly, but she couldn't. Her twelve-year-old field of vision had been too narrow. Sixty-year-old patriarchs just hadn't registered.

She sipped at her wine and then kept her voice casual. "So what happened?"

"He kept right on being generous. When I turned eighteen, he gave me twenty thousand dollars. He had no intention of holding the sins of the father against the son, he said. The money was mine. He hoped I'd use it for college, to make something of myself."

"And did you?"

"Not a chance." Mark laughed, then drank deeply. "I invested in a pharmaceutical company I'd been reading about. I just had a gut feeling it was going to take off, and it did. In a year I had enough to buy my mother a house in Virginia." He refilled his glass. "I finally found time for college when I was twenty. When I was twenty-three, I came back to Moonbird Key, became a partner in the hotel. I've been here ever since."

"Partners with your cousins?"

He nodded. "Phil and Edgerton were having some money troubles, and they were looking for a partner with high liquidity. Luckily I qualified."

She found herself smiling, thinking of Edgerton having to welcome back his "poor relation" as a partner.

"So," she said with a rather heavy-handed irony, "how much did you let them keep?"

He swirled his wine for a moment. She thought she saw a smile tucked into the dimpled corner of his mouth. "Let's see. Phil has twenty-three percent. I think Edgerton kept twenty-six."

She did the math quickly. "Which left you with... fifty-one."

He cut her an amused glance. "I told you I enjoy having control over my finances. And my enemies."

"Which one is this?" She put the question softly.

He stretched his legs out with great deliberation, careful not to jostle the camera. "A little of both, I guess."

"So why don't you leave?"

Setting her wineglass on the windowsill, she turned toward him, kneeling close enough to see his face. Had those years as a dependent really hurt so much that he needed to live in daily intimacy with his revenge?

"Edgerton is capable of running the hotel. Why don't you move away from here?"

He didn't answer for a long time. He seemed to study her with darkened eyes, as if the answer lay hidden in her features. "I suppose it's because the Moonbird has become a part of me," he said slowly. But he wasn't looking at the hotel. He was looking at Glenna. He raised his hand and cupped her cheek in his palm. "Because once you've loved her in the moonlight, nothing else will do."

Glenna stiffened, suddenly frightened by the way her skin flamed under his hand. This could easily get out of control. So much passion flowed from him right now, like a river at flood tide.

And somehow the passion he expressed for stones and mortar, for land and legacy, for beauty and magic—it all became mixed up with these strange new passions she felt blooming inside her.

But they weren't *physical* passions, she told herself nervously, straining her neck to tilt her head away from his hand. They were more emotional. Creative. Academic. She was discovering a passion for color and light, for the sensuality that existed in nature, in the random, unexpected beauty of things. It had nothing to do with sex. It had nothing to do with Mark.

So why…why would her heart beat its wings against her breast when he touched her like this?

Perhaps, she thought desperately, the whole process of awakening her inner eye was confusing—perhaps she was transferring some of the passion to *him*, because he had been the one who brought forth those new, exciting visions.

She leaned back. He followed, bending forward. She couldn't break the connection without leaving the safety of their small, dormered haven.

Suddenly their one shared square of flat roof seemed too tiny—and the sloping fall outside its boundaries was like the fall off the edge of the earth. She pressed herself against the edge of the dormer, but still he followed. She couldn't quite remember how to breathe. The touch of his fingers was so soft and yet it seemed to be the trembling epicenter of all awareness.

When he grazed his thumb along her cheek, her skin burned. When he traced the outline of her mouth, her lips tingled. When he lowered his hand to her neck, her throat ached as if her heart were pounding there.

"Mark, don't," she said. The night had been so lovely. This would spoil everything. "I can't—we can't…"

But, ignoring her words, he reached out and pulled her back to him, sweeping her into the dark circle of his arms, until not a sliver of moonlight could come between them. Her foot slipped on the shingles, and she clutched at his shoulders with panicked fingers.

"Glenna." His voice was husky, amused, intimate. "Relax. I'm not going to let you fall."

But she *was* going to fall. She could feel a terrifying void opening up beneath her. Her heart sped. "This is not a good idea," she said stiffly, hating that stupid, prissy sound, but unable to change it. "I have to check the camera. I have to bracket the expo—"

"Glenna," he said again, pulling her even tighter. He lowered his head slowly. "Shut up."

And then there was no room for words. He kissed her, his lips slanting across hers with a confident possession. His lips—they were wonderfully warm and shockingly hard. Their breaths commingled in a rush of moonlight and wine, an intoxicating blend that made her head feel suddenly light, slightly dizzy.

*Oh, no...* She murmured another protest, more a vibration than a sound, but he didn't release her. He answered with a groan, delving deeper, taking more and more of her until her whole body responded with a deep, moaning shudder.

"I want you, Glenna," he said, lifting his head just far enough to allow words. His eyes glittered in the moonlight. "You must know how much."

"No," she whispered, pressing the heels of her hands against his chest. "No."

"Yes." He tilted her, drawing her all the way across his body, making a cradle of his arm. Or was it a prison? She couldn't seem to escape, couldn't even seem to try.

She met his strangely intense gaze helplessly. The moonlight threw deep, unfamiliar shadows across his strong, wonderful face, painted strangely erotic blue highlights in his hair. He was like a beautiful, dangerous angel of the night.

"You know, Glenna." He put the palm of his hand over her breast and pressed slowly, until she could feel the throbbing of her heart against his touch. "You know because you want me, too."

How could she explain that her heart was racing

with fear, not with desire? Or were the two emotions strangely kin?

She closed her eyes, trying to fight down the pounding as he began to move his hand. He was merciless. He drew complicated patterns of fire across her body—neck, breasts, the clenched plane of her stomach. She tightened with helpless longing as he increased the pressure, circling, tugging, massaging. Her back arched on an agony of sensation as his fingers slipped under her sweater and found the hot skin of her breast.

He worked the wool away from her body, and then, with the softest flash of the most searing fire, he touched the pebbled tip with his lips.

She cried out. It was too much. It was too strong. It pierced her through to the core.

And it mustn't happen. She tried to struggle up, to find herself before she was lost forever. But her body no longer quite belonged to her. She was clumsy, and in her struggles her fingers touched glass. She felt the empty flute behind her rock on its base and knew with a fatal certainty that it was going to fall.

"Mark," she cried as the glass went tipping end over end down the slope of the roof.

He lifted his head just as the last glimpse of shimmering translucence plunged over the edge, coming within an inch of the camera.

There was a breathless silence and then the distant, pitiful sound of shattering glass.

She looked at him, horrified, aware that foolish tears filled her eyes. He tightened his arm around her shoulders.

"It was just a glass, Glenna," he said, his voice as tense as his body. "Don't try to make it an omen."

But it *was* an omen. She knew it. And he knew it, too. The knowledge was a deep black emptiness in his eyes. She felt an answering hollow where her heart used to be, and her tears wouldn't stay where they belonged. They seeped out, trickled down, ran heedlessly onto his fingers.

"No," he said more harshly, brushing the tears away with rough fingers. He gripped her shoulders hard. "Don't cry. I don't ever want to see you cry again. The damn glass means nothing, Glenna. Do you hear me? Nothing."

"Yes, it does," she said, pulling herself free. She fumbled with her sweater. "It means I shouldn't be here. It means this is dangerous for me." She managed to make it to her knees, shaky but intact, pressing her back against the opposite corner. "It means that *you* are dangerous for me."

"Dangerous!" His jaw tightened, and he ran his hand viciously through his hair. "For God's sake. Do you imagine for one minute that I would hurt you?"

"I don't imagine," she said simply. "I *know* you would."

He stared at her a long moment, but he didn't contradict her. Something twisted in her chest, pinching off her breath. She knew what that meant. He didn't answer because he knew she was right. There was obviously nothing left to say.

"Then go," he said flatly. "Go now, before I change my mind."

Mark wandered along the boardwalk at Miller's Landing, wondering what in hell he was doing here. Checking out the possibility of buying this waterfront shopping village was nothing but a fool's errand.

While the place had a certain rustic-Florida charm, as an investment it was so rotten you could smell it three counties away.

The little problems alone were enough to kill the deal. Parking was inadequate, the neighborhood was ratty, a quarter of the retail space was boarded up and half of what remained was the worst kind of tourist trash.

But there were big problems, too. The developers had built far too close to the water, and their construction was cheap and shoddy, nowhere near sturdy enough for hurricane territory. The quaint, rickety boardwalk might survive a category three, but bring another category five like Andrew through here and the whole place would be nothing but a giant pile of quaint Florida kindling.

That might be a good thing, actually. When it was built ten years ago, Miller's Landing displaced about a thousand nesting pelicans.

Mark scooped up a discarded beer can and lobbed it into one of the gaudy trash cans, which apparently were here largely for decoration. Jesus. He'd love to know how *this* zoning variance got pushed through. No way was he going to let the Connelly Corporation get mixed up in this. Coming here had been a fool's errand all right. Which actually was rather fitting. Because, after last night, there was no disputing it: he was the biggest goddamn fool in the entire southeastern United States.

And he might as well be honest. He had come to Miller's Landing because he didn't want to be on Moonbird Key. He didn't trust himself on the same island as Glenna McBride. Hell, he'd be safer if they weren't on the same *planet*.

He bit into his tuna sandwich as if the damn thing had offended him. Another reason he hated this place. They sold lousy food.

But he was avoiding the real issue. What on earth had he been thinking last night? What demon had possessed him to kiss Glenna McBride? For the past ten years or so, his love life had been dominated by one simple rule. He didn't chase women. Ever. He didn't entice, seduce or otherwise conspire to corrupt. Ever.

He'd learned early on that he'd sleep better if he steered clear of wide-eyed virgins. And he'd discovered that there were plenty of women willing to do all the chasing for him. For the most part, those bolder women were tough enough to take whatever they got.

Or didn't get.

And yet, over the past three days he had violated both the letter and the spirit of that one crucial law. He couldn't blame Purcell—the old matchmaker couldn't have guessed that Mark was Mr. Wrong incarnate. And he couldn't blame Glenna, either—she had made it clear from the start that she wanted no part of him.

The moment she arrived on Moonbird Key—perhaps even before that—Glenna had erected a fortress around herself. *Keep Out* signs were everywhere. He'd seen them and he could have, should have—ordinarily *would* have—kept on walking.

But had he? No way. Like a bully on the beach, he had sauntered right up to the fragile little sandcastle and systematically kicked it to bits.

*Nice job, Connelly.*

At least, thank God, he had come to his senses before it was too late. When he had seen those two tears rolling down her cheeks—tears that seemed to come from nowhere, tears as pure and sweet as glycerine, sparkling with reflected moonlight—something inside him had gone a little crazy. He hated it. And he hated himself for causing it.

He wasn't even really sure why he found it so unendurable. He was perfectly accustomed to weeping women—hell, there was one prominently featured in every grand finale of every relationship he'd ever had. He'd seen buckets of manipulative tears, oceans of angry ones and about a million that were equal parts injured pride and thwarted plans.

But he wasn't sure he'd ever seen tears of pure sorrow before. All he was sure of was that he didn't ever want to see them again.

So he wouldn't, that was all. He just wouldn't get close enough to risk it. No problem. He threw what was left of his tuna sandwich to the circling seagulls and, yanking his keys from his jeans pocket, headed back to his car.

Let Purcell deal with her. Yes—that was the answer. It was safer for Purcell. He was eighty years old, for God's sake, and obviously some kind of surrogate father. He wouldn't be tempted to...

To make her cry.

# CHAPTER SIX

GLENNA paused at the entrance to the Moonbird marina, wishing she would trip on the planks of the dock and break her toe. Or maybe just knock her head hard enough to wake up with a massive case of amnesia.

Yes, amnesia sounded good. She'd like very much to forget that she was supposed to spend this afternoon on a boat, roaming the waters around Moonbird Key with Mark Connelly. Maybe if she slipped and hit one of these pilings...

A fat brown pelican squatting on the nearest pole glared at her down the expanse of his ridiculously long beak, as if warning her not to try anything dumb with *his* piling.

She sighed. "Okay," she told the bird. "So what I *really* want to forget isn't where I'll be this afternoon. It's where I was last night."

The pelican didn't even blink. Apparently he had heard far more shocking confessions than that in his day.

"All right," she admitted wearily, as if he had tortured the information out of her. "*All right.* What I *really* want to forget is that I kissed him. And that I liked it."

The pelican just stared. He probably had concluded that she didn't have a single fish on her anywhere and therefore wasn't worth humoring. Maybe if he pretended to be a wood carving, she'd stop jabbering at him and go away.

Finally she smiled at him, amused by his sublime indifference to her petty woes. "Well, it's clear that *you're* not the moonbird," she said half-wistfully, wondering when she had started having conversations with birds. "You haven't the least interest in drying my tears."

The pelican turned his head away, unwilling to dignify that remark with so much as a glance, and began to preen his feathers. *Humans*, the gesture said. *What a bunch of babies*.

And he was right, of course. She was making a lot of fuss and bother over nothing. Today, out on the boat with Mark, everything would be fine. Absolutely fine. Just because she had kissed him last night didn't mean she couldn't work perfectly comfortably alongside him this afternoon. Just because she had briefly lost her grip on reality up there on his roof didn't mean that she couldn't get her feet back squarely on the ground today.

And surely he wouldn't still be angry. Would he?

Granted, he had sounded fairly disgusted last night with her immature dithering, her ungraceful retreat from the delightful tumble he clearly had anticipated. As she had walked back to the hotel, she had felt his dark gaze boring uncomfortably into her from his second-story vantage point, following her progress every step of the way.

But surely he wouldn't hold a grudge. Why should he? That kind of casual sex was probably as readily available to Mark Connelly as a fast-food hamburger. If one door was locked, another one was always open right down the street.

She straightened her back, slipped her camera strap over her neck and started walking down the dock toward the slip that held Mark's boat. She could do this. It was going to be fine.

To her surprise, all three Connelly men were aboard the small, sleek runabout. Mark was fiddling with the engine. Philip was rooting through the hold. And Edgerton was sitting in the helm chair, irritably slapping a rolled-up newspaper against the control panel.

"Hey there, Glenna!" Philip spied her first and he waved eagerly. Well, at least she was assured of one wholehearted welcome.

Mark looked up then, too. "Morning," he said pleasantly. "I see you've met Confucius."

"Who?" Glenna frowned.

"Oh, for God's sake, is that blasted bird back?" Edgerton groaned, then belatedly remembered his manners. "Good morning, Glenna. Don't worry about Confucius—it's not your fault. Mark's made a pet of the stupid beast."

Glenna turned around in time to see the "stupid beast" draw his head high up into an elegantly scornful curve. If she thought the bird had given *her* the cold shoulder, she hadn't begun to appreciate the eloquence of a pelican's body language. The look in his round, pale eye was positively baleful as he stared Edgerton down.

"He's named Confucius?" She lifted her head, reappraising the bird.

He accepted her scrutiny haughtily, then spoiled the effect by waddling comically toward the boat. He stopped at the edge of the dock and stared at Mark, opening his impressive mandibles wide to reveal his empty pouch.

"Go away, you shameless beggar." Mark glanced up, and a smile tugged at his lips. "There's no food on board today."

Confucius closed his bill slowly, as if to express his profound disappointment in Mark. He eyed them all in turn and then waddled ponderously over to Glenna. One of his wings slid at an unnatural angle toward the dock, dragging along the planks.

She bent down, distressed. "Oh, I think he's hurt," she cried. She reached out, wondering whether she dared to touch the injured wing. "Mark...his wing."

To her surprise, Mark didn't even look up. "His wing was fixed years ago," he said disgustedly. "Knock it off, Confucius." But the pelican, apparently deaf again, paid no attention. Sighing, Mark scrounged around in the cooler and came up with a small can of sardines. "All right, you old faker, come and get it."

His hearing miraculously cured, the bird hurried over to the boat, his short legs duckwalking energetically. Sure enough, his wing was tucked back up where it belonged. Glenna laughed, oddly delighted.

Edgerton didn't seem to see the humor. "I've been waiting for you to get here," he told her somewhat sharply, his manner that of a truant officer.

Glenna felt her back stiffen at the tone. Really, he was an officious man, wasn't he? He wanted everything around him to run like clockwork, no time wasted, no nonsense with the stupid birds and beasts.

It suddenly occurred to her to wonder if she had maybe been a little like that over the years, too. But she didn't have time to explore the thought because Edgerton was already barking out his next question.

"I need to know when Mr. Jennings is going to be well enough to start taking pictures again," he said.

"Not to belittle your skills in any way, Glenna. I'm sure they are quite adequate. Good, even."

She smiled around clenched teeth. *Good, even.* How generous of him.

"But, you see, the publishers did promise us that Purcell Jennings himself would be taking the pictures of the Moonbird. We've opened our entire hotel up to him. So I'm sure you can see why we're eager to have your publishers keep their end of the bargain."

He tried that slick politician's smile on her, but it made her nerve endings bristle. If she'd had feathers like Confucius, they would all have been standing on end.

"Of course," she said politely, struggling against a strong desire to see him ground into pelican food. "I'll convey your concern to Purcell."

Mark was adjusting the dials on the control panel. "Have you ever seen any of Glenna's photographs, Edgerton?" He put the question idly.

Edgerton frowned. "Of course not," he said. "You're the one who's been escorting her around the past two days, not me. Where would *I* have seen them?"

Mark didn't look up from his study of the radar. "Well, she had a photographic essay in *Gulf Coast Magazine* two months ago," he said casually. "And she's contributed to a couple of pieces in *Architectural Digest* this year, as well. And she does a lot of free-lance travel work. The local paper has used her several times."

Edgerton looked shocked. But he couldn't have been any more surprised than Glenna was. Mark had just recited her entire print credits for this calendar year. If he mentioned the Koenig wedding and the O'Malley christening, she would probably faint.

"Wow." Even Philip looked amazed. "Great going, Glenna. Very impressive."

Good grief, she thought, embarrassed. Had they assumed that she'd never even seen a camera until two days ago?

"I'll show the photos to you when we get back to the hotel, Edge," Mark continued in the same conversational tone. "They're really quite exciting. Purcell may have been around longer, but Glenna's eye is fresher. She has a particular feel for the sensuality of nature."

The *what*? Glenna looked at Mark with a wide-eyed astonishment.

Sensuality? What on earth was he talking about? She thought over the pictures he'd mentioned. All black and whites...one Mediterranean-style celebrity bedroom, one pretty standard dawn-over-the-ocean mood piece, one strangler fig and one downright lucky shot of a finger of heat lightning dipping into the Gulf.

All in all, nothing that remotely qualified as "exciting". But she understood that, in spite of last night, Mark was defending her, and she was grateful. She tried to catch his gaze, to thank him with her eyes, but he was bent over the radar, still apparently absorbed in his work. Well, there would be plenty of time to thank him while they were out on the water together. Perhaps, while she was at it, she might even apologize for last night....

Philip's head was in the cooler. "Hey, Mark," he complained, "no beer in here?"

"No liquor on my boat," Mark said calmly, finally finished with the radar. "You know that, Phil."

"Well, it's just the runabout," he muttered. "It's not like you're loaning me the cruiser."

Mark raised his brows. "No liquor."

Mark was loaning Philip the runabout...? For a short, uncomfortable moment, Glenna tried to misunderstand. But she couldn't. Mark was already stepping off the boat. He had his denim jacket under his arm and was tossing the keys to Philip. Glenna just stood there, watching mutely.

Finally, for the first time today, Mark looked straight at her.

"I have to go over the Miller's Landing figures with Edgerton this afternoon," he said. His eyes were unreadable, and after a few seconds he slipped on his sunglasses. "So Phil offered to take you out instead."

She had been wrong, she realized—he *was* angry. This was a deliberate brush-off. He wasn't planning to discuss anything with anybody. He was just getting rid of her.

"Great. That's fine," she said stiltedly, willing conviction into her voice. "Thanks, Philip. It's nice of you to take over for Mark."

Accepting Philip's hand, she stepped onto the boat. Smiling broadly, he led her to a cushioned seat and then went back to start the engine. And as the motor sputtered and choked, filling the air with the smoky sting of engine oil, she turned to look at the dock one last time. Mark still stood there, watching as if he didn't trust Philip with his precious boat. He had draped his jacket over his shoulders, and his dark glasses flashed in the sunlight.

He didn't watch for long. As soon as the engine caught and roared to life, he turned away without so much as a wave and headed back toward the hotel.

Glenna felt a dull flush spread over her face. She had overestimated herself, hadn't she? He never had been angry. Why would he bother getting angry with a silly girl who wept over broken wineglasses and overreacted to a few friendly kisses?

No, he wasn't *angry* with her. He was *bored*.

Two days later, Glenna sat at an umbrella-shaded table by the side of the Moonbird's Olympic-size swimming pool, feeling awkward in her overly warm caftan. It was five o'clock on the afternoon of the official luau, and almost everyone else had stripped merrily down to their swimsuits hours ago. She wasn't really sure why she hadn't joined them.

She had worn her bathing suit under the robe, fully intending to dive right in. But the moment she arrived, she had seen Mark slouched comfortably on a deck chair, already wet and gleaming, his eyes obscured by those familiar, nearly black sunglasses.

He had turned his head toward her, lifted his glasses briefly and offered her a polite but oh-so-remote smile, as if he were greeting a stranger he could just barely place. The moonbird tattoo had flexed slightly as he moved his hand, the way a real bird might shift, reacting to an unwelcome presence.

From then on, she'd felt strangely self-conscious, like a girl whose date has ditched her. That was absurd, of course. Mark wasn't her date—he had barely spoken to her in two days, ever since he had dumped her onto Phil.

But whatever the reason, the reluctant minutes had stretched into hours, and still she couldn't bring herself to shed her caftan.

"This has been a success, don't you think?"

Deanna Connelly, one of the few other fully dressed holdouts, strolled over and joined Glenna at the table. Deanna looked better today, Glenna thought. She had some color in her cheeks, and her eyes were not quite so listless.

"Absolutely," Glenna agreed. She smiled, encouraging Deanna to sit down. They had shared a table at lunch, and Glenna had found that she liked the other woman very much.

"Connelly parties are always successful," Deanna observed, a hint of irony in her soft voice. "The three of them see to that. They set the tone somehow, and everyone else just falls into line."

Glenna looked at the pool, aware that it was true. The Connelly men had such vigor, such charismatic energy, that it was impossible not to share their enthusiasm. Even now, after all these hours, the three of them were still going strong.

Amy was riding Mark's broad shoulders in the shallow end, magisterially demanding that he convey her hither and yon. Philip was sitting on the diving board, tossing a water basketball into a floating hoop. Edgerton was doing laps, his bronzed body shaving through the water like an arrow.

This was the first time Glenna had seen Edgerton without his Armani on, and she was surprised to see that he'd had his tattoo removed. Only a slight speckling of the skin on his forearm even hinted that the moonbird had ever been there.

That was slightly suspicious, wasn't it? Mark and Philip ignored their tattoos as if the moonbird had been there so long it had become as much a part of their skin as a birthmark or a scar. Only Edgerton had apparently found his tattoo so oppressive that it needed to be eradicated.

But perhaps she was grasping at straws. She realized that, in spite of everything, she had begun to hope that it was not Mark's hand she had seen luring Cindy out that night. And surely Edgerton would be a much more likely villain anyway, with his conspicuous weakness for blondes.

But what about Philip? He was making his way through plenty of girls today, too. She watched him, laughing from the diving board as an extremely busty young woman tossed the ball back up to him. He was indulging in plenty of booze, too. That, she speculated, could be a lethal combination. Especially late at night, in the black waters of the Gulf…

She gave up, suddenly wearying of her mental game of Pin the Guilt on the Connelly. It seemed, at least for the moment, utterly pointless. Cindy was gone. Would knowing which Connelly had seduced her bring her back to life? Of course not.

Glenna's head hurt. She wanted to go up to her room. Mark had barely spoken a hundred words to her all afternoon, and she was tired of trying to avoid looking at him.

But the party simply wouldn't end. Several dozen guests lingered, obviously reluctant to miss a minute. Middle-aged ladies with zinc white noses, kids with plastic giraffe water rings and buxom blondes in thong bikinis milled about, laughing and drinking and, often, just watching the Connelly men at play.

One of the blondes, in fact, was spending *all* her time watching the Connelly men. Glenna studied her absently, wondering why she seemed familiar…and then she remembered. The last time she had seen this particular blonde, the girl had been tipsy, shoeless, and dancing in the moonlight with Edgerton Connelly.

And now she was here, draped across the chaise on her stomach, facing the water, obviously mesmerized by the golden flash of Edgerton's triceps as he performed a flawless freestyle up and down the pool.

And all this in front of his wife…

Glenna suddenly hoped he'd miss a stroke, snort an unflattering nose full of pool water and get a terrific chlorine headache. In the meantime, she'd have to distract Deanna. "Living here must be like attending a never-ending party," she said as a waiter passed by with a tray of fruit-laden sweet drinks. "Is that exciting, or does it get old after a while?"

"Well, it's not old yet." Deanna smiled. "During the renovations, things were pretty slow. And, of course, I've been ill so much the past few years that any partying around here has gone on without me."

Glenna murmured something sympathetic, trying not to flush at Deanna's unfortunate choice of words.

But Edgerton's wife must have read the worry in Glenna's face because she hastened to explain, "Well, not ill exactly. Just weak. Edgerton and I have been trying to have another baby, but it's been difficult. I don't seem to… I keep…" She took a deep breath. "I've had four miscarriages in the past three years. It's been very hard on both of us."

Glenna's heart tightened. Poor woman—no wonder she looked washed out. Four in three years? Deanna was studying her fingernails as if she regretted revealing so much.

Impulsively Glenna reached out and put her hand on the other woman's wrist. "Maybe you should quit trying for a while," she said, knowing it was none of her business but unable to curb herself. "Just let your body rest a little."

Deanna looked up and smiled. "Yes. The doctor says we'll have to. For a while anyway. It's very difficult for Edgerton, though. He wants a son so badly."

Glenna glanced at the pool, where Mark was now showing Amy how to do the breaststroke. Why should Edgerton want a son? As far as she could see, he exhibited no interest at all in the child he already had.

As if to prove her point, Edgerton climbed out of the pool and planted himself with exaggerated nonchalance on the chaise nearest to the blonde. Glenna's eyes narrowed. A nose full of chlorine wouldn't quite do it, she thought. She might have to take him out to the swamp and feed him to the alligators.

"Ladies, ladies—this won't do! Everyone must swim!"

Glenna looked up, startled out of her nasty thoughts by Philip's voice. He loomed over them with the same wobbling grin he'd worn at the ball the other night.

"Don't you beautiful ladies want to swim? Or at least come join in the swimsuit competition?"

"Not today, Phil," Deanna said, her voice tight but determinedly pleasant. She exchanged a quick glance with Glenna as if to warn her.

So it hadn't been an aberration, Glenna thought sadly. Philip had a drinking problem. She watched him as he pulled a chair up to their table, saw him swig back the remains of someone's wine, indifferent to good manners and good hygiene alike. She looked away, uncomfortable. What a waste.

"Well, if not today, how about tonight?" He smiled at Glenna. "Mark monopolized you for two whole days, and all I got was one short boat ride. It's still my turn, don't you think? How about we go look for the moonbird tonight? Just you and me."

"Sorry, Phil." Mark's voice was so close Glenna started at the sound. "Glenna doesn't believe in the moonbird."

Glenna looked over her shoulder, and her heart lurched at the sight of him, just out of the water, his hair still dripping into his green, sunlit eyes. He looked so familiar suddenly, the way she remembered him from that summer, that she could hardly bear it.

Even way back then, she had noticed how different he was from his cousins. They seemed manufactured somehow, like pumped-up Ken dolls. Their chests were smooth and hairless, their tans unnatural with their light eyes, their bulk unwieldy, disproportionate, achieved by hours of self-absorbed training. Even at twelve, she had liked Mark's looks better. He had a graceful, masculine body, strong and leanly muscled. His skin was naturally golden, polished by the Florida sun to a high gloss, and dark, crisply curling hair made an interesting V on his chest.

Now he rubbed a thick white Moonbird towel over that chest, and the motion was so unwittingly sensual that she had to look away.

Philip was pretending to pout. "What's this? You don't believe in the moonbird?" He shook his head, scolding. "*Everybody* believes in the moonbird, Glenna."

"Well, I believe in the *spirit* of the moonbird," she equivocated, uncomfortable with the sudden spotlight. "I believe in the moonbird as a—as a symbol."

Mark chuckled. "Glenna's big on symbols," he said dryly. "She likes omens, too."

"Omens?" Philip's eyes widened with exaggerated

interest. He leaned forward, and she could smell the liquor on his breath. "Sounds exciting. What omens?"

"Nothing—none. Really, I—"

"All kinds of omens," Mark explained conversationally, as if Philip had asked him, not Glenna. "For instance, she believes if you break a wineglass, you'll have bad luck."

She glared at him, willing him to stop. But Philip laughed.

"Oh, Glenna, sweetheart," he said. "If you've broken a glass of wine, you've *already* had bad luck." He grabbed a goblet from a startled waiter who was clearing off the adjoining table and raised it to the light. Nothing. He lowered it, disappointed. "Unless, of course, it was already empty," he added irritably. "Then you've just had bad service."

An hour later, it was finally over. Mark and Edgerton had gone off together, deep in conversation; Philip had fallen asleep on one of the chaise lounges; Deanna had retired to her room, pleading fatigue.

Glenna, trying to buy some quiet time for Deanna, had promised Amy that she would go with her to the little girl's "secret place", hidden somewhere on the hotel property. Glenna was to bring her camera so that Amy could take a picture of a bird's nest she had found, but she had to double-dog-swear that she would never reveal the exact location of the secret spot.

Still amazingly energetic after her busy afternoon, Amy chattered all the way down to the nature path. Glenna let her hold the camera, and she clenched it in her little hands, right in front of her chest, like a fragile birthday cake. She looked down at it constantly as she walked, as if to reassure herself that it was still there.

"Did you see me swim, Glenna? Mark was teaching me the breath stroke. He says I'm a very good swimmer."

Glenna smiled. "Yes, I did," she said. "You were great."

"But he still says I can't go out in the Gulf without water wings. Not till I'm older. That makes me mad. He thinks I'm a baby."

"Oh, no, honey, that's not why he says that." Glenna's heart slipped slightly at the thought of Amy out there in that black, heaving water with its angry riptides, its blind cross currents, its undertow that could grab you like a monstrous pair of hands and pull you down. "It's because the Gulf is really, truly dangerous. You should listen to Mark. He loves you and he doesn't want you to get hurt."

"Mamma says I could drown." Amy's lips thrust out in a pout. "Everybody worries about that all the time. Amy might drown, Amy might drown. Well, I'm not going to. I'm a very good swimmer. They don't make a fuss all over Philip, do they? And he doesn't know how to swim at all."

Glenna cast the little girl a hard, curious glance. "Your uncle Philip can't swim?"

Amy shook her head. "No. He's scared of the water. I'm not allowed to push him in the swimming pool, even."

Glenna stared ahead of her into the thicket of trees, behind which the island sun was still blazing brightly, though it hung deep in the western sky. Her mind was strangely, helplessly blank, as if it had no idea how to process this information. Philip couldn't swim?

"Did he *used* to be able to swim?" She felt uncomfortable, pumping this child for information. "A long time ago?"

"Never," Amy said with all the scornful assurance of a five-year-old. "I don't see what he's afraid of. *I* learned to swim when I was a baby."

But Amy hadn't even been alive ten years ago. Wasn't it possible that Philip acquired his fear of the water on that fateful night? Perhaps what he witnessed that night that had shown him firsthand exactly how terrible the sea's power could be.

But... She tried to sort it out. If his fear predated that night...well, then what? Then he couldn't have been Cindy's partner. Because she had seen Cindy climb out the window, Glenna knew that her sister had been wearing her swimsuit. When her body was found, she had been naked.

The swimming wasn't just an impulse of the moment. She had *planned* it with someone, someone whose arm bore the moonbird tattoo.

But if it couldn't have been Philip...then that left Glenna with only two suspects.

Edgerton. And Mark.

No, she admitted reluctantly. It really left her with only one. Her heart just wouldn't let her believe that Mark's was the hand that led Cindy to her death. She had no real reason for eliminating him, except that something deep inside her rejected it. That same hand, those same long fingers, had touched her, had stroked her skin...

No. No. It simply couldn't have been Mark.

"Hi, Mrs. Levenger. Hi, Mr. Jennings. Glenna and me are going to take some pictures."

Amy's high, happy voice broke into Glenna's thoughts, silencing her mental thrashing. To her amazement, Purcell and Maggie were walking along one of the branches of the nature path, clearly returning from the beach. They carried a picnic basket between them.

"Hi," she said numbly, wondering if her brain had somehow overloaded, blown a fuse.

Hadn't Purcell decided to skip the luau because he was feeling weak? Hadn't he said he'd be resting all afternoon? What was he doing here, now? With Maggie. In shorts and a baseball cap. Purcell didn't wear shorts...

"Hi, Glenna." Purcell's face was deadpan, offering no explanation. "Going swimming? Water's great. Quite restorative, in fact. I feel fifty years younger."

Maggie laughed, that low, intimate chuckle that seemed to be her specialty. "Only fifty?" she murmured.

Why, the old devil. Glenna looked from Maggie to Purcell in astonished silence.

"No, we're not going swimming," Amy piped up, unaware of any adult nuances. "We did that at the luau. Now we're going to take pictures." She looked worried. "But it's a secret. We have to go alone."

Maggie and Purcell exchanged a glance of wordless amusement. "Oh, well, I guess we'll just have to find something else to do," Maggie said blandly. "If it's a secret and all..."

"It is." Amy was getting impatient. She looked at Glenna expectantly.

Suddenly a loud noise, a man's deep voice raised in some strong emotion, broke through the momentary silence. The three adults glanced at one another curiously, though Amy seemed too absorbed in her own plans to pay much attention.

The sound came again. Glenna glanced around, strangely uneasy. She thought she recognized that angry, barking voice. And then, off in the distance, she saw them—two men, two familiar forms silhouetted against the low-riding sun.

"Oh, my." Maggie had seen them, too. Her face tightened. "Oh, dear."

It was Edgerton and Mark, and they were clearly in the middle of a blistering argument. Glenna thought quickly. She had to get Amy out of here.

She bent down, ready to tell Amy that they must leave. But somehow, for some crazy, self-destructive reason, she didn't want to abandon the two men to their own wild tempers. Perhaps, she thought, if the men knew they had a witness, it might keep things from spiraling out of control.

But Edgerton's own daughter mustn't be the witness. Glenna decided she would stay, would try to see what she could do. But Amy must leave.

She spoke quickly before she could have second thoughts. "Amy, honey, I need you to do a favor for me." Amy looked up, curious but ready to cooperate. Glenna smiled. "I forgot the telephoto lens back in my camera case. We're going to need it if we want photographs of the baby birds. Mr. Jennings knows where I keep it. Will you go back with him now and get it for me?"

She glanced up at Purcell, who nodded immediately, his expression thoughtful and somehow understanding. Glenna was suddenly intensely grateful for his keen perceptions. She knew he would see to it that locating the lens took as long as possible.

Amy's nod came more slowly. "Well, okay, I guess so. Are you going to wait here for me?"

"You bet," she promised. "Now hurry—we don't want it to start getting dark."

Maggie offered Glenna a sympathetic smile. "Good luck," she said softly, and then she turned to Amy. "All right, miss," she said. "Let's hit the dusty trail."

Glenna didn't wait to watch them go. She had dispatched Amy just in time—the argument between the two men was clearly escalating quickly. One of them was shouting now, shoving at the other one. She instinctively began moving toward them, not sure what she could—or even should—do. She only knew that she had to try to intercede.

The path wound circuitously through the hotel grounds, and when Glenna was directly opposite the men she stopped. If she followed the paved path, she would wind away from them—but to reach them she would have to climb through yards of dense tropical plantings.

She looked down at her bulky caftan, wondering whether to shed it.

"You goddamn hypocrite."

It was Edgerton's voice, but it was full of more vitriol than she could have imagined he possessed. She could hear every word now, with painful clarity. She gathered the hem of her caftan together and lifted it, freeing her legs.

"How dare you preach to me? Mark the heartbreaker. For God's sake, man, you bed a new broad every other Sunday."

"This isn't about me." Mark's answering voice was deep, harsh, laced with fury that was no less deadly for being under a rigid restraint. "I can have a different woman for breakfast, lunch and dinner every day of the week if it suits me. I'm not married, remember? I don't have a family.''

"Well, I don't have much of one, either," Edgerton retorted, his voice poisonous. "What do I have? A wife who's too sickly to do anything but weep and sleep, and a kid who—"

But he never got to finish that terrible sentence. Glenna heard the dreadful sound of a blow, bone slamming against bone, followed by the crash of a body falling heavily onto the thick underbrush of palmettos and ferns.

She dropped her caftan, horrified and, for the first time, frightened. This was too dangerous, too powerful—like a runaway train. Her insignificant presence couldn't stop it.

But as she stood there, paralyzed, Edgerton came barreling through the undergrowth and onto the path right in front of her. He was holding the bridge of his nose, and a red trail of blood zigzagged from his nostrils to his chin. When he saw her, he hesitated, unsure for once how to handle the situation. But it was too late for "handling". That she had overheard the men was obvious—she knew it was written all over her face. She could hardly look at him after what he had said about Deanna and Amy.

He narrowed his eyes, obviously reading her contempt accurately. For once, he was too angry even to think about practicing a politician's damage control. "Looking for my cousin, Ms. McBride?" His voice was distorted, but the sarcasm was withering nonetheless. "Well, I'm sure he'll be delighted to see you."

She didn't move. She was still half-frozen from shock.

"Don't be afraid—he won't hit *you*," he said.

"Everyone knows you're the flavor of the week." He smiled unpleasantly. With the blood trickling around the edges of his lips, the sight was gruesome. "Something of a change for our boy, though, aren't you? He usually goes for the more exotic flavors. I don't think he's ever picked old-fashioned, uptight vanilla before."

She flushed, but refused to respond.

He shrugged. "But hell, what does he care? It's only for a week."

# CHAPTER SEVEN

As SOON as Edgerton rounded the corner and vanished from sight, Glenna bunched her caftan around her thighs and cut through the crushed ferns and broken palmettos, looking for Mark.

It took a minute to find him. He stood quietly, deep in the spreading shadows of an ancient banyan tree, with one shoulder against the complicated tangle of auxiliary roots. He was staring out toward the Gulf.

If she hadn't known better, she might have thought he was calmly admiring the setting sun. It was worth noticing—it had slid even lower in the sky and was spilling an intense orange glow across the surface of the water.

But the subtler signs told a different story. He was unnaturally still, and his body emanated such tension that the area around him fairly hummed with it. His gaze never blinked, and somehow she knew he was blind to the beauty before him.

Worried, she drew a little closer. The few beams of light strong enough to pierce the tree's canopy caught him from the side, spotlighting the squared set of his jaw, the narrowed glint of his eye. He was almost a stranger.

She bit back a gasp. The passion that had driven him to hit his cousin was undoubtedly still cooped up inside him like a living thing. What willpower it must have taken, she realized, to stop after only one punch.

She paused then, suddenly unsure of herself. She had rushed to him instinctively, believing he might need a friend, sensing somehow that violence did not come easily to him. But now that she was actually here, she felt foolish. Why should he welcome her intrusion into this family matter? He had done nothing in the past two days to indicate he even considered her a friend.

She backed up a step. She wasn't aware of making a noise, but obviously his system was primed and on the alert. He whipped around, turning that stiff stranger's face toward her.

"Glenna." His voice was altered, too, as if his effort to control his temper had flattened all the pleasing resonance out of it. "What are you doing here?"

"I came to see if you were all right," she said, launching right in for fear he would try to send her away. "I heard you and Edgerton arguing. I saw him leave."

His nostrils flared as he took a deep breath. "How much of it did you hear?"

"Not much."

"How much is 'not much'?"

She hesitated. How could she translate all those ugly words into more civilized phrases? Instinctively she decided to omit Edgerton's accusations about Mark's revolving bed. "I gather that he…he seemed to think you had no right to criticize his…life."

"Well, that's certainly the expurgated version." He titled his head. "And did you happen to hear exactly which part of his life I had dared to suggest might be slightly problematic?"

"No…" She braided her fingers around one of the aerial vines that dripped from the banyan branches. "Well, I mean, I assumed it must be the blonde. The one he was…dancing with."

"Sleeping with," Mark corrected coldly. "The dance was imprudent, but in this part of the world, dancing rarely leads to blackmail."

"Blackmail?" For a moment, she had to steady herself on the vine. "My God. She's blackmailing him?"

He laughed, and, like his voice, it was an altered sound. "Well, you must have missed the best part. That's right. Blackmail. This enterprising young lady has decided that her silence on the subject of Edgerton's sexual antics ought to be worth roughly fifty thousand dollars."

"My God." Maybe it was another sign of her naïveté, but Glenna was appalled. Extramarital affairs were bad enough, but she had innocently believed that the young woman must be infatuated, dazzled into indiscretion by Edgerton's sophistication, his suave good looks.

Blackmail, though—that took things to a new level. The lowest level.

Surely, she told herself, Mark wouldn't have any part in such a sleazy transaction. Maybe that was why Edgerton had been so furious—because he couldn't get Mark to participate in the cover-up. Mark would tell him to face the music…take it like a man.

Or would he? She looked at his dark, shadowed face uncertainly. What did she know about him, really?

Maybe, when the chips were down, the Connelly boys still stuck together. They certainly had ten years ago, after Cindy's death. She remembered how the three of them had arrived at the police station together for questioning. And how they had left together, too, as free as the moonbirds they wore on their wrists.

Perhaps cover-ups were the Connelly specialty.

"So what is he going to do?" She watched him carefully, hoping she was wrong.

"He's going to pay." Mark snapped a twig in two and tossed it to one side. "Rather, *we're* going to pay. Edgerton never has that much spare cash. That's why he came to me. For a loan."

Her heart drifted down, down. "Oh," she said because she couldn't think of anything else to say. She had to get out of here. It was late. The sky was so orange it seemed to be on fire. She made a vague gesture toward the path she'd left behind. "Well, I'd better be getting back. I'm sure you can take care of it for him…make sure he gets away with it." She stopped, feeling her voice tremble with smothered anger. "I really must go."

"Goddamn it, Glenna." Mark's brows were knitted in a fierce frown, and he stared at her through narrowed eyes. He grabbed her arm roughly. "Don't do this."

She paused. "Do what?"

"Don't judge me by Edgerton's behavior. Don't make me carry my cousin's sins—believe me, my own are heavy enough."

"I'm not—"

"Yes, you are. You're blaming me because you think *he's* a bastard. Well, damn it, so do I. You think he ought to pay for his indiscretions. *So do I*. You think he—"

"*I* think he ought to be flogged in a public place." She met his gaze squarely.

Mark didn't flinch. "So do I."

She shook her head. "I guess the only difference, then, is that I wouldn't pay a cent, not one single dirty penny, to protect him from the consequences of his actions."

Mark sighed. "Neither would I."

She made a small, impolite sound of incredulity. "You just said that you were going to pay—"

"Not to protect Edgerton, Glenna." Mark's voice softened slightly. He had begun to look and sound more like himself. "I'm willing to pay to protect Deanna. And Amy."

She looked at him, suspicion warring with her desire to believe. "Don't you think Deanna knows that her husband strays, Mark? No wife is that blind."

"Of course Dee knows there have been women. But she doesn't know *this*." A look of sheer revulsion passed over his features. "At least I hope she doesn't. This girl has no conscience. And she has some pretty ugly details. Places, preferences…some really sick stuff. You've seen how fragile Dee is. Would you be able to let her read details like that in the papers if a few thousand dollars could spare her?"

Glenna hesitated. The edges of her comfortable indignation were blurring. She looked around them helplessly, as if the twisted banyan tree held the answers to all the bewildering moral ambiguities of life in its hundreds of intertwined arms.

"I don't know…I don't know what to think."

"Then just trust me."

She shook her head. How could she? What did she really know about him, except that he made her nerves tingle, her heart ache, her senses overload? And apparently he did that to all women—a new one every breakfast, lunch and dinner, every day of the week. He had certainly done it to Cindy.

"Glenna? Glenna, where are you?"

It was Amy. Glenna looked toward the path, dismayed. She had promised she'd be waiting for the little girl.

"I'm just over here," she called. "Wait there, sweetheart. I'll be right out." She turned to Mark, who still held her arm. "I have to go," she repeated quietly.

His fingers tightened briefly, then finally relaxed and slowly set her free.

"Goddamn it, Glenna," he said, his voice low, throbbing with an angry frustration. "What have I ever done to you? Why the hell can't you just trust me?"

It was four in the morning, and Glenna was out on the beach, trying to find something to photograph. She had walked around for an hour, her camera loaded with her familiar, reliable black-and-white film, searching the moonlit darkness for one of those perfect arrangements of lines and angles that used to thrill her so. Or one of those geometric shadow patterns, perhaps—silver on jet, coal on pearl—that she once had found so fascinating.

But there was nothing. Nothing. She forced herself to shoot an entire roll, but she knew that none of it was even worth developing. Dead things, like drifts of turtle grass. Trivial things, like the white-lace trim at the edge of the Gulf's black satin petticoat. Hollow things, like the ruined perimeter of yesterday's sandcastle.

Nothing. The water rolled slowly onto the sandy shore, its rhythm tired, its tone sibilant, slumberous. She had lost her feel for all of this....

She lowered herself wearily onto the nearest of the long line of comfortable double chaise lounges. She had even tried photographing them, thinking that the large, domed beach shells attached to the head of each one might look mysterious, as if ghosts were lurking in the hooded shadows.

But she knew already that the picture had failed. The moon had slid behind a cloud, and the light wasn't right. She dropped her camera into the case and wrapped the edges of her beach blanket around her shoulders. She had lost it, just as she'd lost the comfortable sense of order and restraint that had sustained her for the past ten years.

She had lost that the minute she set foot on Moonbird Key.

"Sneaking off to take pictures without informing your assistant?" Mark's voice suddenly came from nowhere, from the shadows…from the dunes…from the Gulf… She couldn't tell. Her heart reacted to the sound by hammering at the wall of her chest.

"I suppose I assumed all potential assistants were safe in bed," she said, attempting a small smile. She pulled the blanket tighter around herself, as if she feared he might be able to hear the clamor of her heart. She wondered how he had known she was here.

"Not tonight," he said. He came around the foot of the chaise and stepped into her range of vision. The moon chose that moment to shake off its cloud, and Mark appeared to have been carved in silver light. "I guess you weren't the only one who couldn't sleep."

Still huddled inside her blanket, she studied him. He didn't look as if he hadn't slept. He looked wonderful. His white cotton shirt was crisp and pristine. His old, soft jeans glowed like deep blue moonlight.

She shifted a little toward the shell that covered the head of the chaise, seeking the safety of its shadows. "What's keeping you awake? Is it Edgerton? Has anything gone wrong with..." She didn't know what to call it. "With the deal?"

He turned his face toward the hotel. "The deal is done," he said flatly. "I gave her a check for fifty thousand. She left. That's all there was to it."

"Oh?" She eyed him quizzically. "Well, for a man who has just vanquished the enemy, you don't sound very pleased."

"*Pleased*?" He turned back to her. "How in hell could you think I'd actually be pleased to be a part of this sick, underhanded..." Her eyes widened, and he ran his hand roughly through his hair. "I'm sorry," he said dully. "I'm not saying any of this right. I keep forgetting that you can't know how much I hate this. I keep forgetting that, in spite of everything, you don't really know me very well."

"No, I guess I don't." She looked over at him, at his handsome face, wondering how he could have come to matter so much to her so quickly. She *wanted* to know him, to understand him, to believe him, but... "How could I?" She shook her head helplessly. "You aren't like anyone I've ever met before."

"But that shouldn't make it harder to know me, Glenna," he said. "In some ways, I'm probably the most straightforward man you'll ever meet."

"No," she said quietly. "That's not true."

"Yes, it is." Turning away, he paced off several restless steps, then strode back to where she waited. He seemed to have come to an important decision. "Glenna, I want to tell you something about myself."

He sat beside her on the chaise and touched her

knee. She shivered. The wind had picked up, and the night was turning cold. Even in Florida, winter nights could chill you to the heart. She brought the blanket up to her chin and edged farther into the shelter of the beach shell.

"You don't have to tell me anything," she said. "I shouldn't have been so judgmental about Edgerton this afternoon. What you do is really none of my business."

"Isn't it?" Though his head was limned in silver, his eyes were in shadow. His gaze was inscrutable. "Anyway, I didn't say I *had* to tell you. I said I *wanted* to."

She nodded, strangely reluctant to open the door to intimacy any further. It was as if, once cracked, the door could never be shut again. "All right."

He took a deep breath, then sighed and began to talk.

"A couple of months before I was born," he said, "my father was caught embezzling money from the Moonbird accounts. He had lied and cheated and stolen from the people he loved most, and he was banished because of it. After he died, my mother told me what had happened. She watched me like a hawk for fear I'd show signs of being like him. When we came back to the Moonbird, my uncle watched me the same way." He paused. "I lived my life in the shadow of those mistakes, Glenna. I vowed that I'd never repeat them."

"Oh, Mark," she said inadequately. "How terrible." Suddenly she understood what he had meant the other night when he referred to "the sins of the father". Old Mr. Connelly had taken him in, but he had never let him forget that he didn't really belong.

Mark shook his head. "No, don't be sorry. In a strange way, it's been very freeing. No one trusted me, so I had to trust myself. I've developed a habit of saying what I mean and doing what I think is right. I've become my own judge and jury. Mostly I don't give a damn whether other people approve of me or not."

He looked at her, one brow raised in that quizzical expression she was coming to know so well. "But for some crazy reason I cannot decipher, I *do* care what you think. That's what's kept me up all night, Glenna—remembering the look on your face when I told you we were going to pay the money. God help me, I need to make that look go away. I need you to understand why."

"Mark," she began. But suddenly a strange, throbbing noise broke into their intensely private world. She gasped, then subsided as a flight of black skimmers beat past in formation, searching the calm night water for fish. When she looked back at him, his face was intense, dark, completely serious.

"I'm not a perfect man, Glenna, but I am an honest one. I barter only in truths, even the bitter ones. I don't lie for personal gain or to escape paying the price for what I've done. But that's a private, personal decision. I don't insist on heralding my version of the truth from every tower if it's going to destroy innocent people."

"Like Deanna."

"Yes," he said. "Like Deanna." He leaned in very close, as if he needed to see the expression in her eyes. They were both under the hood of the beach shell now, and he put his hands on her forearms. "*Can* you understand? Can you trust me, Glenna?"

"Yes," she said, and suddenly, miraculously, it was

true. Her doubts were somehow being subdued by the passionate candor she could hear—could almost *feel*—in his voice. She felt it in his fingers, saw it in his eyes. "I do. I understand. I trust you."

She took his hand, turned it over. With her forefinger, she slowly traced the subtle lines that she could barely make out here in the dim shadows of the beach shell. The moonbird.

He allowed her silent scrutiny patiently, bemused but accepting, waiting for her to explain. She tilted his forearm into the moonlight, bringing the tattoo to life. She rubbed her thumb over it, experiencing it with a new sense of wonder. This was not the dangerous moonbird of her dreams, but the brave protector of the legend. Her beautiful moonbird.

She lifted her eyes to his and, as the last mists of doubt beautifully cleared away, she could finally recognize her own blinding truth. Somehow, somewhere, between ten years ago and tonight, plain, old-fashioned vanilla Glenna McBride had fallen in love with this sensuous rebel, this exotic, erotic and hopelessly unattainable man.

"Mark," she whispered, bringing the moonbird up to her face, holding it against her lips. "Oh, God... Mark."

"Yes, my love, yes," he said, surging forward to take her into his arms. His voice was strained, husky in the night air. He groaned as he folded her against him, brushing her hair back from her eyes. "Yes, look at me like that. That's the expression I've been waiting to see on your face ever since the day I met you."

She turned her face to him like an offering. Whatever it was he could read on her features, whether it was her longing or her love, her fear or her fire, it was his. She wanted him. That was not new—she had always wanted him. He had offered her tantalizing glimpses into a secret, sensual world that had so long been closed to her. A world where love and need were as intertwined as a strangler fig and its host. Mated, unto death.

But, until now, she had been too much afraid, and always she had turned away. Tonight, everything was different. She wanted him, but she loved him, too. It made everything right, everything worth risking. If only for tonight, she wanted to see through his eyes, feel through his fingers, know through his heart. Letting the blanket fall away from her shoulders, she took his hand and placed it over her breast.

The pleasure was rich, thick, intense. He was so warm. He let his hand slowly soften, until the palm seemed to fit against her as if it had been molded for that place.

"I want you," he said simply, just as he had the other night when they had last touched like this. "I want to make love to you. Do you trust me enough to let me do that?"

She nodded. She trusted him with her body, with her heart.

"I'm going to want it all, Glenna." His voice was insistent. "If we make love, there will be no holding back, no safety net. Are you ready to let go? Are you ready to let yourself relinquish all control?"

She looked at him, her breath stalling. His eyes were lasered pinpoints of light in the center of a bottomless darkness.

"Think about it, sweetheart," he said. "You will have no control. Do you trust me enough for *that*?"

She was having difficulty breathing deeply. Something heavy and hot seemed to have filled the lower half of her body, and her lungs had no room to expand.

"No control," she echoed huskily. "Yes. Please, yes." She heard the small whisper of cloth as he slipped loose the top button of her blouse. "We can... my room..."

"No." He moved to the next button. "I want you right now. Right here."

She felt her heart trip hard against his hand. "Out here?" She swallowed. "But we're so... Someone might... Isn't it...dangerous?"

"Yes," he said with a dark, quiet emphasis. "It is."

He had undone all the buttons now, and he pulled the fabric away from her skin. The cold air closed over her, and her midsection clenched in a spasm of surprising heat.

"I *want* it to be dangerous," he said, touching her breasts with his hands, running his fingers over the nipples that had hardened painfully under the slow chill of the wind. "I want you to take that risk with me."

He lifted her, eased her out of the shirt. A strange panic was tightening to agony inside her. She didn't know what to do. He clearly wasn't going to be satisfied with a quick, furtive fumbling under layers of protective clothing. He was going to strip away all her defenses, open her to the night. And to him...

He lowered his hand to the waistband of her jeans and tugged slowly at the zipper. She tried to be calm, but every muscle in her body screamed with tension. She couldn't. She just couldn't. Someone might see. Someone might walk along the beach just as she had. Someone might watch from the windows of the hotel.

She reached up and took his fingers in both her

hands, begging him soundlessly to stop. "I can't," she said finally, and the sound was more a moaning than real words. "I'm afraid."

"Of course you are, sweetheart," he said, pressing the heel of his hand against the aching heat between her legs. "Don't fight the fear. Let it in. Let it be a part of the desire."

She tried—oh, how she tried. Her hands still trembled, but somehow she made them loosen their grip on his fingers. *No control.*

"That's my girl," he said softly. He didn't wait for her to grow accustomed to the decision. He slid the zipper open and tugged the soft denim across her hips.

More cold air. More cruel coils of tension. More impossible gasping fear.

"Help me," she whispered. "I don't think I can do this."

"Yes, you can," he murmured, rocking his hand gently, making the ache stab and retreat, stab and retreat, until she thought she would cry from the amazing, yearning pain of it. "You *are* doing it."

And then the jeans were there no longer. Moonlight touched her everywhere with cold white fingers. Every muscle in her being burned with the need to bend, to curl, to hide, to protect. But she fought the terror. She lay open to the night, battling for breath.

"Oh, yes, my love, my brave, sweet love." He kept one hand against her trembling body, but his other had left her, working quickly at his own buttons. "We're almost there."

She had thought it might be easier when she was not alone, when his clothes, his own defenses, were discarded, too. But instead it was worse, because when she saw him, she knew that there was no going back, no retreat to safety, no last-minute change of heart.

His thrillingly, terrifyingly male body was going to possess her. He would be the first, and he was going to do it here, with the full moon watching them, with danger pressing in from all directions.

The sky was losing the deep, black-velvet emptiness. Silver-rimmed clouds began to make themselves seen, and in the sky above his shoulder she saw a hint of gray. Oh, no, the dawn...

She moaned, biting back words of fear. She wanted to tell him to hurry—they mustn't linger. But she knew it would do no good. *He* was in control. *His* hands held the leash that chained the danger. He intended to let the beast come much, much closer before he pulled it back.

He lowered himself over her slowly, sliding his body against her aching skin, trailing kisses. Sliding down, down, until his head was poised above the shadows between her legs. He touched her softly with one finger. When he spoke, his breath was hot against her, and she trembled.

"You've made it, Glenna. Can you feel it? The desire is riding bareback on the fear."

"Yes," she whispered. "Yes."

"And now we must find the place beyond the fear." He let his finger slip inside her. She whimpered at the strange rush of heat, the weird, arrhythmic ripples that shuddered through her. "It's beautiful, Glenna. *You're* beautiful."

He touched his lips to her then, and she cried out into the night, forgetting fear, forgetting danger, forgetting everything except the deep, spiking pain and the desperate straining toward release. She clutched at his hair as her body arched, stretched to the breaking point.

Her breath began to come in small, agonizing pants, and then he rose again. He lifted himself over her, and she could feel the hot hardness of him, his body thrusting, seeking, needing.

He held back one last time. "You do trust me, don't you, Glenna?"

She nodded, beyond words. She lifted her hips, opening her body in unconditional surrender to whatever was to come.

"It will hurt," he said softly. He pushed, and she gasped, stunned by the splitting, searing tension. "Don't fight it. Just ride it, like the fear."

He pressed harder. Her body wept, and she did, too. He held her gaze, and she clung to the sight of him through her tears.

"Trust me, my love." He began to move inside her. "Nothing can harm us now."

He drove harder, passion finally breaking free of its leash, ripping apart the cords of his self-control. She gripped his shoulders as, for a single, bloodred moment, pain and fear and desire combined into one, and she thought she might drown under their terrible power.

But then, suddenly, there was no pain, no fear, only the most exquisite tidal wave of pleasure. She cried out his name as the stars broke into a thousand sparkling splinters that shot through the night.

Stars raining on his shoulders, still he rode her, rode the rising, cresting swell of her, until he cried her name, too, on a long and shuddering groan.

And then she knew nothing, except that the tidal

wave had broken, flooding them both with a force that seemed to sweep away the darkness, leaving behind only a wet and gleaming, silver-coated dawn.

# CHAPTER EIGHT

SHE could have stayed there forever, she thought, lost in that shadowy world between sleeping and waking, between dawn and daylight, between passion and its price.

Only one minute—maybe two, she thought, two very short, stingy minutes—had passed before they heard the distant sound of running, of an early-morning jogger's shoes slapping against the damp sand.

Her heart leaped crazily.

"Shhh..." With one fluid motion, Mark dragged the edge of the discarded blanket up. One snap, and it billowed over and around them, settling against her skin like a warm cocoon. He spooned his body behind hers and nuzzled the back of her neck.

The footsteps flew by, never skipping a beat. The sound stretched away down the beach, fading to silence.

Slowly her shivers subsided. Had the blanket been there all along? She had forgotten it. But *he* hadn't, she realized, not for a single moment. It had been only a flick of his fingers away. He could, at any time, have covered her in an instant.

She smiled to herself, ducking her head into her shoulder. He had never let the danger come so very close after all, had he? Not close enough to hurt her.

"If you let your hand fall over the side, your fingers will touch your clothes," he said softly, his breath whispering against her neck. "The blanket will cover you while you dress."

To her surprise, in spite of the night's cataclysmic changes, in many ways she was still the old Glenna. Dawn had brought an unexpected shyness, a reluctance to openly acknowledge what had happened in the night.

But, of course, she had no choice. She couldn't just lie there naked forever.

She dispensed with as many extraneous items as she could, but still the act of dressing this way was strangely erotic. He watched from smoky eyes as she shifted under the blanket, wriggling into her jeans, sliding her legs one by one, lifting her hips...doing everything slowly, awkwardly, by feel alone.

Finally she was decent—sort of. All critical areas were covered, though most of her buttons were still undone, and she still held a handful of lacy white underthings that she hadn't quite been able to manage.

"Thanks," she said politely. She sat up, turning her back to him, and addressed the buttons.

She should have known he wouldn't bother writhing around to dress in the shelter of the blanket. He tossed back the blanket, swung his legs over the side of the chaise as if it were a bed and stepped into his jeans with an easy practicality that turned out to be the quickest method anyway.

He stood, his bare feet and bare chest looking somehow completely natural in the silver dawn light. This was his element, she thought as she watched him stretch lazily and yawn. He was wild and he would never be fully tamed, whether he was waltzing in a moonlit ballroom or making love by a starlit sea.

And would she *want* to tame him even if she could? She hesitated. The noble answer was no, of course.

But the truth was not quite so selfless.

How could she honestly say that she wouldn't love to own such a man? Who wouldn't want to possess his laughter, his power, his sensuality, his easy acceptance of the world and all its miracles? Who wouldn't want that body beside her every midnight, every dawn, from now until forever?

But if anyone ever did manage to domesticate this tiger, was it really going to be plain, vanilla Glenna McBride? She saw how absurd that sounded, a million-to-one chance. And she had never been much of a gambler.

As he slid his arms into his crumpled shirt, he turned to her with a smile, and the smile alone had the power to make her blush. "I'll walk you up," he said, pulling the shirt's edges together and fingering the buttons deftly.

"No." She shook her head. "It would be...less obvious if we didn't come in together."

"Would it?" He chuckled warmly, as if she amused him in a most pleasant way. "Okay, if it makes you more comfortable to think so."

She knew what that low laughter meant. She touched her hair, suddenly realizing that her French braid had unraveled hours ago. The once-pristine grosgrain ribbon now hung like a limp white strand of seaweed over her shoulder. She flushed again. She was probably a walking neon sign that said "sex" in large red letters. Looking down, she fidgeted with her tennis shoes, retying both perfectly good bows.

"Damn it all, I have to be in Fort Myers all day," he said, and she realized that he had come up behind her, one leg kneeling on the chaise. He put his hands on her shoulders. "I can't avoid it. I'll be back by nine." He kissed her neck. "Can you wait that long for dinner?"

She stared straight ahead, waiting for the goose bumps to die down.

"Dinner?" She tried to sound lightly playful. She didn't want him to hear the very real anxiety buried beneath the teasing. "But I was your breakfast treat, wasn't I? Surely you'll be wanting a new flavor for dinner."

He laughed out loud. "I knew you'd overheard that comment, you little Puritan."

"Of course I heard it." She lifted her chin. "You and Edgerton were yelling so loudly I suspect they may have heard it in Fort Myers."

Laughing, he pulled the pitiful ribbon slowly from her hair. "Hmmm... Well, I think I must have forgotten to mention that sometimes..." He brushed her hair away from her ear and bent his lips to the lobe. "Sometimes, when I find a flavor I really, really like..." He nibbled at the soft skin, sending trickles of pleasure down her spine. "Then I just want to have the same thing over and over. Again and again."

Somehow she kept her head erect. "Until you've had enough?"

She felt his lips curve in a smile against her ear. "That's right, sweetheart. Night after night. Until I've had enough."

Glenna left a message for Purcell, asking whether he wanted to go over proofs with her before lunch, but thankfully he never called. Picnicking with Maggie Levenger, no doubt. But Glenna was too tired to care. As soon as she had showered and changed her clothes, she dropped onto the bed and slept until well past noon.

Perhaps it was from having been up all night, then sleeping the day away, but when she woke up, everything felt slightly unreal. She wondered, for a strange, dislocated moment, whether she had created last night out of the fevered ethers of a dream.

Her thoughts circled themselves, chasing each other pointlessly like horses on a carousel. Even if she could believe it had been real, what had last night really meant to him? Would he come tonight? The night after? How long could she hold his attention? Wasn't it just a little too crazy to hope that a man like Mark Connelly might choose a lifetime of vanilla?

And even more troubling, what would his reaction be when she told him who she was—and why she had really come to Moonbird Key? Because she *did* have to tell him. As he had said, he bartered in truths. Even the bitter ones. So if they were ever going to build anything more meaningful than a one-night stand, it was going to have to be built on the truth. The whole, tragic truth.

The afternoon passed slowly. No matter what she did, the sense of floating in limbo just wouldn't go away. It was, she thought, like being poised in the expected path of a hurricane. Everyone knew hurricanes were unpredictable. One might veer off and miss you altogether. But it might sweep into your life and completely rearrange the landscape.

All you could do was wait and see.

Around four o'clock, desperate to distract herself,

she wandered out to the beachside café, which was normally almost empty at that hour. She was surprised to see Deanna and Amy sitting at an umbrella-shaded table, both looking quite elegant in their designer jeans and silk shirts.

They beckoned her over with eager smiles.

"We're looking at maps, Glenna," Amy said, noisily waving a huge, creased piece of crackling paper at her. "We're finding good places to visit. *I* like the sound of Timbuktu, don't you?"

Glenna considered. "I don't know," she said. "It sounds far."

Amy scowled, clearly disappointed in her. "That's what Mamma said." She tried to flatten the map against the table, making more crackling noises. She ran her stubby forefinger along Australia, searching doggedly. "Well, it doesn't sound far to me. Except I just can't find it."

Glenna and Deanna exchanged smiles over the little girl's head. Exasperated, Amy moved to an empty table nearby, where she could spread her map out for better hunting.

"Planning a trip?" Glenna asked as the waiter brought her a cup of coffee, unbidden. Ever since the day of her crazy lunch on the seashore, the waiters had all treated her like a minor celebrity.

Deanna nodded, fiddling with a gold bangle that just cleared her violet-silk cuff. "I thought Amy and I could use a little time alone," she said quietly, watching her daughter with worried eyes.

Glenna wasn't sure what to say. Physically, Deanna looked almost completely restored. Her dark hair glowed, and her brown eyes were as deep and lustrous as a Gypsy princess. She looked just about ready for that tiara after all.

So why the sudden interest in "time alone"? Was it possible she had finally tired of Edgerton's indiscretions? Or had she somehow heard about the payoff to the blonde? Glenna decided to say very little for fear she might say the wrong thing. But it didn't matter. Deanna was clearly ready to unburden herself to someone, and Glenna was elected.

"I'm afraid it might be hopeless to keep trying to make it work," she said softly. "They just weren't made for marriage."

Glenna sipped her coffee, adopting a similar casual tone. "Who?"

"All three of them!" Deanna sighed. "They're all the same. Of course, Phil and Mark have had the sense to stay single. But Edgerton has the same need for variety, for constant stimulation. He never should have…" She twisted her huge, square-cut diamond. "He never should have married. I honestly think it just isn't in the Connelly nature."

Glenna looked out toward the sun-sequined Gulf, struggling to keep her face serene. If only Deanna knew how desperately she did *not* want to hear this. She fought the craven urge to stand up, make some excuse, flee from this voice that was putting words to all her own secret fears. She even wondered whether Deanna might have guessed how she felt about Mark. Perhaps Deanna meant her comments as a warning.

Glenna shook herself, took a bracing gulp of coffee. That thought was paranoid—and rather shamefully self-centered. Of course Deanna didn't know how Glenna felt about Mark—she hadn't given it a thought. Right now, she was coping with a crisis that threatened her life, her marriage and her family. She was just hungry for any sympathetic audience.

"I guess it doesn't help that they are so diabolically attractive," Glenna said with a gentle smile. "Women always falling at their feet... It would take a saint to resist all that temptation."

Edgerton suddenly appeared at the edge of the restaurant, looking as handsome and immaculately groomed as ever. Even the small, flesh-colored bandage across the bridge of his nose was discreet and tasteful. He smiled as he spotted his wife and moved to join them.

"Yes, it would take a saint." Deanna smiled back grimly. "And unfortunately there's not a saint in sight." She sighed, pushing back the glossy curve of her hair with beautiful, newly manicured fingers. "Although I suspect that lately I've been doing a pretty good impersonation of a martyr."

Oh, yes, Glenna thought, Deanna had definitely begun to regain her self-esteem. Her husband had better watch out.

When he reached them, Edgerton kissed his wife and daughter, but to Glenna's surprise, he addressed his first words to her.

"I owe you an apology, Glenna," he said in a self-effacing tone that was so effective she caught herself half-believing its sincerity. "I was unforgivably rude to you yesterday. It's no defense, but I can only say that I've been under a lot of stress lately, with the campaign and...everything. I spoke a great deal of nonsense and I am truly very sorry."

Glenna hardly knew what to say. She would have liked to believe that he had gotten quite a scare from his blackmailing blonde and had decided to turn over a new leaf. But this was Edgerton. He'd have to turn over a whole new *forest*.

She didn't hold out much hope.

"Don't give it another thought," she said politely, unable to summon up much warmth. Deanna might be a pushover for her husband's blond surfer-boy good looks, but Glenna's personal weakness was for something darker....

"I found it!" Amy's voice rang through the nearly empty restaurant with a triumphant glee. "It's in Africa. In the Sahara Desert. Can we go there, Mamma?"

"We'll see," her mother said noncommittally. And then, as Edgerton went to look at Amy's discovery, Deanna turned her lovely, sad eyes toward Glenna. "Maybe I could resist him in the Sahara," she murmured with a soft irony. "That might be far enough."

Glenna smiled, but she knew it wasn't true. Deanna loved her wretched husband rather hopelessly, that much was clear.

And as Glenna had just discovered to her own dismay last night, there was nowhere on this whole crazy, spinning planet where you could really hide from love.

The knock on the door sounded at five minutes after nine. It echoed through the room like gunfire, and Glenna cast one last, nervous look in the mirror.

The sight was dishearteningly ordinary. In spite of the new bright blue gypsy blouse and matching, softly swirling skirt she had bought at the boutique downstairs, she saw essentially the same demure schoolgirl who had looked out from that mirror yesterday.

Apparently, losing one's virginity, however monumental the occasion might be emotionally, didn't really mean one went from Sandra Dee to Marilyn Monroe overnight. She plucked at the scooped, gathered neckline of the blouse and wondered if she might have overestimated her odds. A million to one? Try ten million.

Mark knocked again, and she grabbed a brush, trying to make something sultry and sensual of her long, unstyled curls. While she brushed, she scanned the room quickly. Bed neatly made, drawers all closed, bathroom tidied. She had even remembered to put away the picture of herself with Cindy. Glenna, looking like the mouse she had been called, was unsmiling and nervous next to the golden feline grace Cindy had so naturally possessed.

Mark's third knock came with slow, exaggerated emphasis, as if he knew she was in there, as if he knew she was dithering. Embarrassed, she dropped the brush on the dresser, hurried to the door and opened it.

He was leaning against the jamb patiently, his legs crossed at the ankle, his arms folded across his chest. Her heart stopped. Oh, dear God, she loved this gorgeous man.

"Hi there," he said. His smile was full of teasing intimacy. "Playing hard to get?"

She flushed, pulling the door wide enough to let him through. "It would be a few hours too late for that, wouldn't it?" She tried to smile, too.

He shut the door slowly behind him, never taking his gaze from hers. One eyebrow was arched so high it almost touched the single dark wave of hair that had spilled onto his forehead.

"Oh, I don't know," he said pleasantly. "In fact, this is the logical moment to sound the retreat, don't you think? You know—you could say you've been having second thoughts…it might have been a mistake…it must have been the moonlight…''

A mistake? She fingered the smocking at her gathered neckline, wondering dismally if he was merely voicing his *own* regrets.

''And if I said those things…'' She forced herself to hold his gaze, ordered her chin not to drop, her lips not to tremble. ''What would *you* say?''

He looked thoughtful. ''I'd say you might be right.''

She held her breath as the words slid, rapierlike, under her ribs. Oh, God… She had been wrong. It had been, perhaps, a *hundred* million to one.

He took two steps toward her. ''I'd say maybe what happened last night wasn't really as wonderful as we think it was.''

He tilted his head, watching her, seeming to find her bare neck beneath the cloak of hair, her breasts beneath the blue silk. Her skin began to tingle as he took two steps more.

''I'd say we probably just imagined the excitement, the heat, the pure, scalding pleasure of it all.'' He paused. ''Nothing could *really* have been that perfect, could it?''

Her knees felt loose, as if the joints were made of some material that softened under the warmth of his voice. She touched the table behind her for support. He was right beside her now. She could smell the clean, damp smell of his recent shower, the simple sweetness of the starch the hotel laundry had used to press his shirt.

''And then—just as a test, you understand—I'd say shut the curtains, sweetheart. Don't let the moonlight in.'' He reached around her and pulled the drawstring slowly. The sheer curtains whispered along their rod, floating into place in front of the windows. "And then I'd say kiss me, Glenna." He took her in his arms. His mouth was so near hers she could just barely make out the gentle grin. "And then tell me if what happened last night was a mistake."

His lips touched hers, so gently that at first it was more like the memory of a kiss. A wordless echo, an ever-renewed question. *Was this a mistake?*

She responded eagerly, her lips soft and ready, as if it had been years rather than hours since he had last kissed her. *No. No. Never. She could never regret what they had done.*

With a muffled groan, he slanted his mouth over hers, dragging heat from one corner of her lips to the other and then back again. A slow persuasion, urging her toward the only answer he would accept. *Or this, Glenna? Do you regret this?*

Her body was already answering, melting, molding to his. Warm trickles of sensation moved through her, as if touching awake each separate part of her body. She shifted in his embrace, awareness creating need and need burgeoning into flame.

He answered by closing his arms more tightly, opening her lips with his tongue, exploring the soft caverns of her mouth, seeking, probing, always asking... *Could this have been a mistake?*

When she was completely undone, her limp clinging his only answer, he lifted his head. "Now," he said, his voice still teasing, but as husky as if he had been screaming his question at her rather than sending it throbbing across their joined nerve endings. "What were we saying?"

She blinked, trying to focus on something other than that funny little drumbeat of desire that had begun to pound in the pit of her midsection. Something more practical than the way her lips still tingled, as if he could touch them with his gaze. She had to be more focused. There was something she needed to say, something she needed to tell him....

"Mark," she began. A low tremor shook her words, but she cleared her throat and went on. "Mark, there actually is something I want to talk about. Something you need to know."

He smiled, stroking her hair away from her ears. "More like a thousand things. I don't know your middle name. I don't know your cat's name. In fact, I don't even know if you *have* a cat."

She shook her head, trying not to be distracted. "Mark—"

"I don't know your pet peeve." He kissed her earlobe, then hesitated. "I hope it's not men who order your meals for you, because I've already arranged for room service to send up dinner." He nuzzled her neck. "But it won't be here for at least an hour, so..."

She drew back. "No, really," she said. "Before... before any of that, there's something important I need to tell you about myself."

"Oh, no." He looked crestfallen. "You're not wearing *panty hose*, are you?"

"Mark." It was as if he had determined not to let her get too serious tonight. She couldn't really blame him—she certainly hadn't always shown him her fun-loving side, had she?

But that kind of playful banter would come later...she hoped. First she had to get past the hurdle of the truth. Stepping away from his embrace, she took a deep breath as if to prepare for the jump. She went to the dresser and leaned against it, her back to the big mirror so that she couldn't see either of them in it.

"I'm serious," she said. "This is something we really have to get out in the open before...before we can go any further."

He raised that one, eloquent brow. "You're married?"

He just *wouldn't* be sensible, would he?

"No," she said, frustrated into taking the hurdle early. She could tell her timing was off—she was going to stumble and fall. "No, damn it, I'm not married. I'm Cindy Maxwell's little sister."

The brow didn't budge. His half smile didn't die. But his eyes widened, just a little, and his body froze into its position. It was as if he'd withdrawn into a place inside himself, leaving only a cardboard image behind.

"Don't you recognize the name?" Glenna couldn't quite tell if his reaction was horror or confusion. "Don't you remember Cindy Maxwell?"

"Of course I remember her," he said in a quiet monotone. "But her sister...her sister was just a little girl...." He let his answer dwindle off, obviously realizing how absurd the comment was.

"That was ten years ago, Mark." Glenna spoke softly. "I was twelve."

"My God. Cindy Maxwell. That poor, beautiful girl. And you—you were..." He began to shake his head. "She called you something else." He frowned a moment, then his face lightened. "She called you Mouse."

Glenna nodded, her throat tightening. "You called me Mouse, too. You were very nice to me one day... one day when I really needed it."

He looked far away, lost in the past. "Yes, I remember that," he said with a kind of surprise that they both could dredge up something so tiny. "We were a lot alike back then. Neither of us quite belonged." He looked at her as if really seeing her for the first time. "I knew I had met you before," he said slowly. "I couldn't remember where or when, but I knew. I just put it down to...I don't know exactly. I guess I thought it was some emotional recognition. A rather rare degree of compatibility."

She nodded. "Yes," she said eagerly. "Yes, I felt that, too."

But he looked unconvinced, as if troubled by some note that didn't fit. "Did you really?" He raised that skeptical brow again. "Then why didn't you ever tell me who you were? This doesn't exactly seem like the kind of secret that soul mates would keep from one another, does it?"

She floundered. "I...I guess I just didn't want to cause—"

His eyes tightened. "And your name. If you had said Glenna Maxwell, I might have made the connection. Is your name really McBride now?" Something unpleasant was slowly dawning in his face. "Is that your... My God—you can't actually be *married*?"

"No, no." She hurried to clear that up, hoping it accounted for the tension on his features. "Of course I'm not. I told you I wasn't. I've never even been engaged."

Instead of clearing, his face grew slightly more strained, and she felt the first twinges of real foreboding. She had known this would be awkward, perhaps even unpleasant. But this was her first hint that it might be...fatal.

"What is McBride, then?" His voice was edged in a strange frost. "Your alias?"

She flushed. "What do you mean by that?"

"I would think it's fairly clear what I mean," he said. "Is Glenna McBride just a name you made up so that no one on Moonbird Key would recognize you?"

She looked at him, hating his tone. "It is my real name," she said stiltedly. "McBride is my stepfather's name. He adopted me."

He smiled thinly. "How convenient for you. So much less bother. And, of course, they say that in any deception you should keep things simple. The fewer outright lies told, the safer the whole charade."

Remembering that she had thought exactly the same thing, Glenna flushed. The day when she had arrived on this island, she had been quite relieved that she could remain anonymous without any direct lies. But that day seemed so long ago now, those emotions unrecognizable.

"It wasn't really meant to be a charade," she said miserably. "Not exactly."

He laughed. "No? Why, then, did you never mention that you had been here before? And those questions about deaths at the Moonbird..." He shook his head firmly. "Oh, it's been a charade all right. The only thing I can't quite figure out is *why*."

In the face of his cold disdain, she felt helpless, as if they had ceased to speak the same language. She wished she could make him understand, but her thoughts were as disorganized as bits of broken shells along the sand. No jagged edge ever seemed to fit the one lying next to it.

"I thought I could just take my photographs and

leave," she said. "I never expected things to get... personal."

"You didn't?" His short bark of laughter was caustic. "What was your first clue, Glenna, that things might be going to 'get personal'? Was it our first dance? Our first kiss? Was last night some kind of hint? Did it finally start to feel a little personal when we were actually having sex?"

"Of course it did." She felt her cheeks burn with both anger and shame. "That's why I'm telling you now."

"But what about *before*?" His voice was as tense as a coiled spring. "Did it ever occur to you that I might have liked to know whom I was *really* making love to?"

She looked down at her hands. "I wasn't thinking very clearly *before*," she said tightly. "I was so relieved that you hadn't been the one who took Cindy..."

She stopped herself, but not in time. She saw his mind working to finish her sentence. She even saw the exact moment he put the pieces together. A darkness seemed to fall behind his eyes.

"My God. It was *you*, wasn't it?" He sounded incredulous, as if he had just figured a puzzle out, but the answer was written in gibberish and made no sense at all.

"Me?" It was gibberish to her, too. "What was?"

"Yes," he said, following his internal logic with a dogged insistence. "It was you who told the police, wasn't it? It was you who reported seeing one of the Connelly boys taking Cindy out to swim that night."

She would have answered, but she found herself suddenly mute. She just stared at the tension on his features, wondering how a man full of such sensuality and laughter could so quickly manifest the blackest, deepest contempt.

"It was you all along." He laughed, a disdainful sound. "Poor little Mouse. So insignificant that summer. We never even thought of you." He put his fingers to his forehead, massaging hard. "But why did you do it, Glenna? Of all the boys on the island, why did you point your finger at *us*? Had one of us hurt your feelings somehow?" He seemed truly curious. "Edgerton, maybe? He's always been arrogant, but still..." He shook his head, his logic apparently reaching a dead end. "*Why*?"

"Because it was true," she answered simply. "Because one of you did."

He didn't speak at first. He watched her as if he were trying to read her mind.

"Why?" he asked again, more quietly. "Why do you insist on thinking so?"

"Because I saw a man's hand," she said, wishing she didn't have to think of it all again, see it all again so clearly. Over the past couple of days, she had almost driven the image from her mind for the first time in ten years. But now her skin broke out in goose bumps as the scene began to play in her mind once more.

"I saw a tanned, muscular arm reaching in through the window. Our parents had the room that led right onto the veranda, so if Cindy wanted to sneak out at night, she had to climb through the window."

He was very silent, very still. His listening had a concentrated quality that was almost intimidating. But somehow she forced herself to go on.

"That night, the moon was full, so the room was

very bright. It made Cindy's blond hair look silver. She was wearing her white tank suit—I remember because it looked silver in the moonlight, too. I pretended I was sleeping. It made her mad when I caught her doing things. She hated for me to know her secrets.''

She suddenly felt overly warm, as if she had begun to perspire. She brushed her hair away from her face and tied it around itself in a thick knot at her nape.

"I didn't see the man, so I've never known which one of you it was. I saw only his hand, and hands aren't distinctive enough to distinguish among them. But, whoever he was, he had the moonbird tattoo on his wrist.''

"No.'' The syllable was a short, stunned sound of protest.

She met his narrowed eyes with as much courage as she could muster. "Yes,'' she said. "I saw it, Mark. I saw it as clearly as I can see yours now.''

# CHAPTER NINE

"DID you think it was my hand, Glenna?"

He looked down at his wrist where the moonbird lay like a brand. It was such a little thing, she thought with a numbed sense of detachment. Such a little thing to have caused so much unhappiness.

He looked up. "Did you think it was my hand?" he asked again.

"I didn't know," she said, trying to be as honest as she could. It seemed the only way. But it was more difficult than she had thought, this bartering in bitter truths. "I didn't *want* to think it was...."

He looked down again, flexing his fingers, making the moonbird fly. "But still...you weren't sure."

"How could I have been sure? I was only twelve years old. You grown-up young men might as well have been from another planet. I couldn't begin to separate truth from lies, villains from heroes."

But that wasn't quite true, was it? Even back then, she had sensed that Mark could be a hero. It was only later, when Cindy was gone and there seemed to be no one to blame, that Glenna's bitterness had attached itself equally to everyone whose name was Connelly.

"You had all flirted with her. She talked about all three of you as if you were thrill rides she couldn't wait to buy tickets for at the fair. Edgerton, Philip, Mark...Edgerton, Philip, Mark...." She shook her head. "I heard your names and I saw you smiling at her in that way I knew was reserved for sex, for beautiful girls who had turned eighteen. I was dazzled by the whole thing and eaten up with envy."

She flattened her hand against the table as if she could hold back the hysteria she felt threatening at the back of her voice.

"So how could I possibly judge which one of you was capable of taking an eighteen-year-old girl out in the middle of the night, giving her beer, letting her go into the dark water, water you must have known was dangerous…?"

"That's why you came back, isn't it?" His face was poker straight, as if it had never expressed an emotion in his life. "You came to try to find which one of us it was."

"No," she said. "I came because I work for Purcell Jennings, and he wanted me to help him with this assignment."

She took a deep breath. Bitter truths, she reminded herself.

"But I did—I did think it would be a chance to ask some questions. To talk to some people. Maybe, if I got lucky, even to find out a few things about what happened to Cin—"

"And did you?" The question came zinging at her like a bullet.

"Did I find out things?"

"Not *things*, Glenna. You didn't want to find out *things*. You wanted to find out *one* thing. Which one of us was guilty of murder."

"Murder?" She shook her head violently. "No—"

"Oh, that's right. Not murder. Manslaughter. That's what the police said it would be. Just a little case of manslaughter. Even negligent homicide, if we came clean, if we admitted which one of us it had been." He looked frighteningly dark, profoundly angry. "The police never did find out who it was, Glenna. How about you? Did you find out?"

"No," she said, unsure when, or how, the conversation had taken such an ugly turn. "I found out who it *wasn't*. It wasn't you."

He laughed. "And how do you know that? Is my tattoo different from the one you saw? You studied it last night, just before we made love. Was that what you were looking for, Glenna? Evidence?"

She shook her head. He was deliberately misinterpreting this. "No," she said again, aware that her denials were starting to sound weak, ineffectual, repetitive. "No, that wasn't why I..."

Mark stood suddenly. He jammed his sleeve up his arm, all the way to his elbow, then thrust his wrist out toward her, exposing the moonbird to the diffused light that came through the sheer white curtains.

"Here. Study it all you want, Glenna. Do you have a magnifying glass? We can look for distinguishing marks."

"No," she said stubbornly. "It wasn't your hand."

"How do you know?" He moved closer, brought the moonbird to within a foot of her face. "Look carefully. Could this have been it? Could this have been the hand you saw leading your sister out to her death?"

"No." She didn't want to look at it anymore. She tried to push his hand away, but he was too strong, too determined that she should see. He held it there, unwavering.

"Was it, Glenna?" His voice was insistent,

strangely altered. "It's the right size, isn't it? The right tattoo."

"I don't know," she said. "It could have been." She surrendered, exhausted. "I don't know, Mark. I don't care anymore."

"But I do." He touched her cheek with the inside of his wrist, bringing the outline of the moonbird right up against her skin. "I've lived with suspicion all my life, Glenna. And I don't like the way it feels, especially in a lover." He stroked her cheek lightly, somehow sadly. "I asked for two things from you last night. I asked for honesty. And I asked for trust." He stilled his hand just under her chin, using it to tilt her face to his. "I didn't get either one of them, did I?"

"I trusted you," she said desperately. "I did."

"No," he said. "Believe me, I'm an expert on the subject. If you had really trusted me, you would have told me who you were. You would have told me what you saw that night and you would have asked me whether the hand you saw was mine. You would simply have asked, because you would have trusted me to offer you the truth for answer."

She couldn't fight him. His logic was flawless, his probing into her deepest, most hidden motives too accurate. He knew things she didn't even admit to herself.

"All right," she said on a small, indrawn sob. "Maybe I was afraid—afraid to talk about it, afraid to be honest. Maybe I was even afraid to find out the truth. Trust comes hard after all these years."

She took another deep breath that hitched in her throat.

"But I gave you my love." She looked up at him

through splintered tears. "I *loved* you, Mark. Isn't that enough?"

He let his hand drag down her neck. Slowly, so slowly, until her cheeks flamed.

"No, sweetheart," he said, and somehow the endearment had become a cold, flat synonym for goodbye. "I don't think it is."

Glenna spent the next day in a strange sort of fog. She was busy, thank heaven, so she had little time to brood. She woke early—if her miserable night of tossing and turning qualified as sleep. She rose, dressed carefully, braided her hair tightly. She worked alongside Purcell for a few hours, did a little developing in her room. She spent quite a while on the telephone, double-checking on things back at Purcell's studio in Tampa.

She tried not to think of Mark. But every time she entered her room, her gaze shot toward the telephone, checking to see whether the little red bubble was blinking. It never was. No one called. No one left any messages. The entire Connelly clan, including Mark, might just as well have vanished off the island.

Midafternoon, she began to make arrangements for the shoot at the next hotel on the list. Florida's east coast this time. Bremer's Landing. Well. That looked nice. A much smaller hotel, but kind of pretty...

She stared at the brochure, trying to imagine what it would be like to stay there, trying to believe that there really would be life after the Moonbird. Bremer's Landing had been constructed entirely of shipwreck timber, the brochure stated. That would be interesting, wouldn't it?

She let the pamphlet drop onto her lap. Wouldn't it?

Just before sunset, she wandered down to the marina. All the boats at the very end of the dock were Connelly boats, Philip had told her. Mark had three himself—the tiny runabout they had used for the tour the other day, a forty-four-foot sailing sloop named *Windwaltzer* and a forty-foot motor yacht he called *The Sitting Duck*.

The two big boats were there, she saw, but the runabout was gone. That could mean anything, of course. Or nothing. Still, on the off chance that he might have taken it out—and therefore would be bringing it back in—she loitered on the dock, pretending to watch the sun set.

There wasn't much to see, actually, just a hint of purple bruising behind a towering column of dense gray clouds. Nasty weather, really. The worst kind of winter day in Florida. The air smelled cold and wet, and it had begun to drizzle lightly. Even the ever-present pelicans seemed disgusted. A half dozen or so of them sat on their pilings, plumped against the wind, their heads tucked in, their long beaks propped on their breasts. They managed to look both irritable and stoic.

Glenna wondered if one of them was Confucius. She would have liked to talk to him. That's how far gone she was, she thought with an internal laugh that just barely escaped being hysterical. If she couldn't talk to Mark, she would settle for a chat with his pelican.

Suddenly the dull rumble of an outboard motor carried in on the wind. Glenna peered out over the water. She noticed that one of the pelicans had roused himself, too, raising his neck into an elongated S and staring toward the sound. She tried not to hope too much, but it was hard to settle the ripple that washed through her midsection as the boat drew closer. It was equal parts hope and fear.

It was Mark's boat. She recognized it instantly. But she couldn't identify the people on it—they wore parkas and caps for protection against the inclement weather. Smart people, whoever they were. Her own hair was damp, frizzing in the increasingly heavy rain. Her shirt clung disagreeably to her skin.

But still she watched as the boat came closer and maneuvered into its slip. The pelican seemed interested, too. He hopped down from his perch and paced with a slow, stately, endearingly goofy waddle near where the man was tying off the line, waiting to be noticed.

Two people...a man and a woman, she could tell now. Glenna's chest tightened. What would she say if the woman was Mark's date? She pressed her hands together. How embarrassing to be caught here, haunting the dock like a sailor's deserted doxy, if he had already moved on to someone else. A dish of unwanted vanilla, melting in the rain, when he had already found another flavor?

Finally, after much laughing and gathering of odds and ends, the two people climbed off the boat, shaking raindrops from their jackets. Confucius stopped midwaddle, staring. Glenna suspected her own expression looked similarly stricken.

It wasn't Mark. It wasn't anyone she knew. Two total strangers scurried down the dock, ignoring Glenna and the pelican equally in their dash for shelter.

Glenna looked back toward the little boat, wondering if she could have been mistaken. But Confucius settled the question. He was standing in front of the still-bobbing runabout, one wing drooping weirdly, dragging along the rain-darkened planks of the dock. He looked utterly forlorn.

"Me, too, Confucius," Glenna said dispiritedly. They made a pretty pathetic pair. "Me, too."

The knock on her door was trying to drag Glenna away from a lovely dream. She was dreaming of flying. Confucius was beside her, and there was a sonata playing. She couldn't remember which one exactly, but it was so lovely....

The knock turned into a pounding, and Glenna finally jolted awake, her heartbeat drumming against her throat. What was that? *Who* was it? The bedside clock read 3:14. In the morning. What in the world...?

She hesitated, uncertain whether she should answer it. Who would be up at this hour?

The weather had been dismal when she went to bed and obviously hadn't improved in the intervening hours. She could still hear the wind gusting against the gingerbread trim of the old building, making it whisper and creak. The window was speckled with raindrops that glowed eerily in the reflected illumination of the porch lanterns.

Suddenly the pounding subsided to a low rustle, as if the person on the other side of the door had grown tired. It was a strange, unnatural sound, and Glenna suddenly felt more worried than nervous.

It was someone in distress—that much seemed apparent. Deanna, perhaps?

She rose, pulling on the robe she always left draped across the foot of the bed, hurried to the door and cautiously opened it. To her shock, the man on the other side almost fell into her room as if he had been resting his entire weight against the wood. She reached out, catching his arm at the last minute and steadying him.

She could hardly believe her eyes. It was Philip.

Philip?

If she had feared, even for a split second, that he had been driven there by some amorous delusion, one look at his unshaven face, his swollen, reddened eyes, his spiked and tangled hair, banished the notion immediately. He clearly wasn't in any shape for a flirtation. He was sick. Instinctively she put her arm around him, ready to lead him into the room. At her touch, he sighed brokenly, and she got a whiff of his breath.

No. Not sick. Not exactly. He was horribly, helplessly drunk.

She hardly knew what she should do. Why on earth had he come to her door in such a state? He couldn't have wanted a near stranger to see this. But maybe he was beyond caring, beyond knowing exactly where he was or why.

"Philip," she said quietly. She led him, stumbling, toward the desk chair. "What's the matter? Do you need some kind of help?"

When she had him more or less in a sitting position, she hurried back and shut the door. She wished she knew Mark's telephone number. He would know what to do. Surely the hotel operator would have it. She went over to the phone, but when she picked it up, Philip grew even more agitated.

"No," he said, half-rising from the chair to take the receiver from her hand. "God, no, don't tell him." He began to cry, a horrible, wet and broken sound. "I don't want him to know."

Glenna replaced the phone in its cradle. "All right," she said soothingly, "I won't call anyone. Just tell me what's the matter, Philip. Tell me why you're here."

He looked at her wildly, as if he recognized her for the first time. He put one trembling hand out and touched the tip of her braid, which lay across her shoulder. "Cindy," he said. His mouth worked, and his eyes squeezed shut as if from pain. He dropped his hand heavily. "Oh, God, God, help me. *Cindy...*"

Glenna recoiled, stunned by the sound of her sister's name on this man's lips. She stared at him, trying to make herself think clearly. But she felt as addled as he was. Her own thoughts were reeling drunkenly now, too.

He had begun to mutter, his head bowed, his whole body hunched forward as if he had doubled over after a blow. Only a few of his words were intelligible.

"Oh, God, God," he moaned toward the floor, over and over and over. "Oh, God, I'm so afraid. *Cindy...*"

"What about Cindy, Philip?" Glenna's voice sounded stiff, strange to her own ears. But even as she articulated the question, she knew the answer. She knew. Finally, after all these years, she knew.

*My God*, she thought, unconsciously echoing the lamentation of the poor, lost man in the chair. *My God, it was Philip!*

"So sorry," he said unevenly, slurring the words. He didn't seem to be able to hold his head up. "Oh, God, so sorry, so sorry..." He put his hands in his hair, squeezing the temples. "So ashamed."

It was unbearable. She found herself patting his arm, murmuring soothing words. "Philip, calm yourself," she said softly, wondering where the impulse to comfort him came from. Wondering where all her anger had vanished to. After all these years of waiting for this very moment, of dreaming of the day when she could make the villain pay... Why did she feel only this rush of pity, this instinct to protect? "Please, Philip." She tried to pry one of his hands from his temple. "Don't torture yourself so."

"Cindy's gone," he said to the floor. "I'm sorry. I can't find her, I can't, I can't..." His voice escalated, rising to a high, frantic pitch. He stood up, every muscle coiled. He seemed driven by some invisible terror. He stared at the door.

"Philip..." Glenna tried to hold his arm, but he was beyond the reach of her voice or her touch. He began to shake his head as if trying to deny some truth too terrible to accept.

"No, no, no, no..." He lurched toward the door and somehow managed to get it open. He turned toward Glenna one more time, and his eyes were almost lucid. "I couldn't find her," he said, and then he was gone, pulling the door closed behind him.

The telephone had rung ten times, but still she didn't hang up. Wedging the receiver between her shoulder and her ear, she dragged on yesterday's jeans and shoved her arms through an old shirt, uncaring that the clothes were worn and wrinkled. They were the only things she could reach from where she stood, and she wasn't going to put the phone down until he answered. He had to be there.

Finally, somewhere around the twentieth ring, Mark's voice came on, thick with sleep and out of sorts. "Hello?"

"Mark." She exhaled his name on a sigh of relief. "It's Glenna."

Immediately his voice sharpened. "Glenna, what is it? Are you all right?"

"Yes, I'm fine," she lied. She could hardly launch into a recitation of her broken heart and its attendant miseries right now. Right now, no matter how her heart ached at the sound of his voice, she had to focus on the immediate problem. "I'm calling for Philip," she said awkwardly. "I mean, because I'm worried about Philip."

"What?" He seemed astonished by her words. "Did you say Philip?"

"Yes," she said. "He's—well, he's been drinking a lot and he's very upset. He was just here—"

"He was in your room?" He sounded incredulous and slightly annoyed as if it wouldn't take much to tip him over the edge of anger. "Philip was in your room?"

"Mark, listen to me." She clutched the receiver in both hands. "He was up here just now. He was crying and he seemed kind of confused. Desperate. He kept talking about Cindy and how sorry he was. How he couldn't find her." She heard her own voice cracking as she relived that shocking moment of revelation. "It was Philip, Mark. The hand I saw that night—it was Philip's."

A long silence greeted her announcement. Then his voice broke it, clipped and curt—and oddly unsurprised. "Where is he now?"

"That's why I'm calling," she said. "I'm worried about him. When he left here, he seemed—wild."

"Where was he going?"

She shook her head though she knew he couldn't see it. "I don't know. I honestly don't know. He wasn't making much sense." She hesitated. "Was I right to call you? I thought someone should know and somehow I didn't want to call Edgerton...."

"No, you were right to call me." He was all business now, trying to rush her off the telephone. "Thank you for that. I'll take care of it from here."

"What are you going to do?" Though she knew she had to, though she knew that even seconds might be important, she didn't want to let him go. She didn't want to lose the comfort of his voice.

"I'm going to find him." He had begun to sound impatient. "Goodbye, Glenna."

But she couldn't leave it that way. "I want to come. Mark, please. I want to help."

"You can't help," he said coldly. "Stay in your room. I'll take care of this."

She did stay—for at least a minute. She stayed long enough to slide her feet into her sneakers, long enough to finish buttoning her shirt. Long enough to find the key to her room and slip it into her pocket.

And then she went off to find them.

She made her way down the elevator and quietly out of the hotel, instinctively heading for the path between the Moonbird and Mark's cottage. He couldn't be more than a few seconds ahead of her, could he?

Though the rain had stopped, the air was heavy with moisture, and the wind, still high, was blowing through the trees in gusts, occasionally shaking a barrage of drops from the leaves and fronds like liquid gunfire. She was wet within seconds. She pushed her hair away from her face. She couldn't see him. The path, lit by the landscaping lights, appeared to be empty. She cursed under her breath.

He had been too quick for her. It was her fault. She shouldn't have bothered with shoes. And why had she looked for the key? The front desk could always have given her another.

Mark undoubtedly hadn't dawdled over such trivial things. Of course he hadn't. He wasn't like her. He didn't let stupid conventions distract him, keep him from doing the things that really mattered.

But where was he? Where could he have gone so quickly? She scanned the grounds, trying to read his mind, trying to intuit what he had been thinking. He had sounded rushed, his voice clipped from the urgency to end the conversation. His tone was as close to fear as she had ever heard it get.

He was dreading something, she realized, something potentially dangerous. But what? What could possibly threaten his cousin here? Where at the lovely Moonbird Hotel did Philip's danger lie?

Her breath stalled. The water. Of course, dear God, of course. The danger waited, as it had always waited, in the water.

# CHAPTER TEN

SHE tried to swallow, but her heart had risen so high in her throat that she could hardly force it down. Her fingers and feet felt numb, but she forced her legs to run, to churn over the path down to the beach. Her shoe had come untied, but she didn't care. She ignored the wet slap of the laces against her bare ankle. She stumbled only once, when she hit the too-yielding sand, but she recovered quickly and began to run again.

*Mark...* She reached the firmer, wetter sand at the shoreline and began to race in earnest. Where was Mark? She scanned the tide line, but saw nothing. She moved her focus out a little farther to where the growling waves were tumbling over themselves, breaking prematurely, lathered by the wind.

He had to be there. She couldn't be wrong. She just couldn't be.

And then she saw him. He was only a few yards out, but he was moving fast, his long, lean legs cutting through the foaming waves, going deeper with every step.

"Mark!" she called his name with all the breath she had left in her lungs. Swerving, she began to wade into the cold, choppy water, too. "Mark!"

She was up to her knees before he heard her. Her

foot twisted on something unseen, and her untied shoe came loose and was swept away by the undertow.

She kept going, kept calling. "Mark!"

He turned, and his face looked furious. "Glenna," he yelled over the pounding surf, "goddamn it, Glenna. Go back."

"I can't," she cried. "I can't leave you. Let me help."

"Go back," he bellowed. "For God's sake, Glenna, go call the paramedics. I can't worry about both of you at once."

And then, finally, she saw Philip. He was still several yards ahead of Mark—dangerously far away. He was up to his shoulders, and with the wind whipping the waves, his head disappeared horribly every few seconds.

"*Go!*"

Glenna was frozen with terror for just a moment, and then, forcing the panic back, holding it at bay with an iron will, she obeyed him. She struggled out of the water and back up the beach toward the undulating row of little dunes. She kicked off her one remaining shoe and ran with all her heart.

The hotel suddenly seemed so far away, like a sanctuary that keeps receding in a nightmare. She kept her eye on the Moonbird, ignoring the way her jeans clung with clammy caresses to her skin, ignoring the hot paths her tears dug as they streamed down her face. And somehow she began to close the distance.

Terror nipped at the edges of her control, but she banished it. She refused to let anything enter her mind except three simple words that she chanted over and over like a prayer.

*Please, save them. Please save them.*

She must have looked appalling. The hotel clerk already had his hand on the telephone, ready to call the emergency number, when Glenna made it to the desk. He handed her the receiver, dumbstruck with horror himself. She wondered if she, too, might be suddenly mute, her vocal cords frozen with fear. But she began to speak, and in a voice that was amazingly coherent—even competent—she told the dispatcher everything she knew.

And then, in case the paramedics were too slow, she told the clerk to summon hotel security. Though her legs burned to run back to Mark, she waited because she *had* to wait. She had to show them exactly where to go. And all the while, she chanted her three words like a mantra, like a charm. *Please*, she prayed. *Save them.*

God must have been listening. By the time she got back down to the beach, the security guard at her heels, Mark was already hauling Philip to the shore.

He let the body drop just clear of the incoming waves, and then, sinking to his knees, he bent his beautiful, weary body over his cousin. His bare back and arms rippled with straining, bulging muscles as he struggled to revive him. He listened, he breathed, he pressed. He refused to let him die.

Every move he made was its own kind of prayer, Glenna thought, blinking back the fractured stars of her tears. Every touch, every exhalation driven into the unconscious man's lungs, spoke of an unearthly determination and devotion.

Perhaps it was the moonbird, she told herself, her exhausted, terrified mind pushed to odd fancies as she watched helplessly, trying to catch her breath, trying to endure the fear. Yes, it was surely the spirit of the moonbird that moved through Mark right now, the self-less love of a strong, beautiful creature as he worked tirelessly to protect the helpless....

Even when the wailing, blinking ambulance came screaming onto the beach, Mark continued to struggle with Philip's body. He worked without looking up until the moment the paramedics took over, placing their hands over his, asserting their belief that medical training was more important than love, that tubes and masks could work miracles that desperation only dreamed of.

Finally, just when she had begun to give up hope, Philip coughed, then groaned and rolled his head to one side. A tiny movement, just an inch...but the most important inch in the world. The inch that was the razor's edge, the line between life and death.

Glenna sank to her knees then, relief robbing her of the tension that had allowed her to go on standing. She buried her face in her hands as they moved Philip onto a stretcher and loaded him into the waiting ambulance. She felt her tears begin to fall again as she heard the doors close, the engine rev, the wheels dig spinning ruts into the wet sand.

She knew without looking that Mark was in that van, too, that as it sped away toward the hospital, it was taking him away from her. She listened until she could no longer hear the call of its siren, and then, finally, she lifted her head.

Mark was gone. And the dawn was still hours away.

Thirty minutes or so later, showered and dressed, with her suitcases packed and waiting in the hotel lobby, Glenna once again stepped onto the sands behind the hotel.

She was early. Another hour remained, perhaps, until the dawn would break, pouring its pearled light onto the black waters of the Gulf. But she had to be here; she had to witness that dawn from beginning to end. It was the last one she would ever see on Moonbird Key.

Like a fickle lover, the storm had completely passed. The wind was a gentle breeze, and the waves were smaller now, quieter, like rowdy children who have been chastised and are slightly ashamed of their earlier excesses. Glenna's white cotton dress, which she wore loose and unbelted, rippled softly against her skin.

The last dark hour before the dawn. This was the hour, more or less, they always said, at which Cindy met her death. And Glenna had come here now to say goodbye.

In spite of everything, she was glad she had come to Moonbird Key. In one short week, she had learned so many things, things she might never have learned in a lifetime of safe existence anywhere else.

Most importantly, she knew, finally, what love felt like. She knew that it made you sing and it made you bleed—but that either way it was too wonderful to miss. Strangely she didn't regret a moment she had spent with Mark—even though she would never have any more moments, even though she would spend her life missing him. She had even learned that she could survive a broken heart.

And she had learned that she really had no taste for vengeance, that bitter, lonely emotion that had once seemed paramount. She had always pictured this day—the day when she could finally prove whose hand had led Cindy to her death—as a day of triumph, a day to sit back and savor the fruits of her revenge.

She had even, in her darkest moments, envisioned taking her proof to the police, perhaps—glorying in the public downfall of a wicked man. Exacting payment for all that the man had taken from her.

But reality had been so different. No sense of triumph had accompanied the revelations. The sight of Philip, his sweetness destroyed, his innocence lost, his conscience ravaged, had not brought her even the briefest microsecond of pleasure. It had, strangely, only made her think of him as one more victim of that awful night.

And, looking at Philip, she had suddenly realized that she hadn't ever *really* been seeking revenge at all.

She had been looking, instead, for peace.

Deep inside, she had always blamed herself as much as she had blamed the phantom hand that bore the moonbird tattoo. She could have stopped her sister from going, but she didn't. She had said nothing. She had carried that guilt a very long time.

Well, she had forgiven Philip last night. This morning, she had to forgive herself.

And somehow she did. As the first creamy glow lit up one corner of the horizon, she finally let go of the last lingering scars of her guilt.

For a minute, she thought she heard Cindy's melodic laughter on the breeze. She could almost hear her teasing approval. "It's about time, Mouse," she almost heard her sister say. "It's about time."

In the silence that followed, Glenna heard soft footsteps on the sand behind her—real ones, belonging to... She whirled around, her heart knowing who it was even before her eyes could prove it.

It was Mark.

He had not taken time to shower or change. He must

have come straight from the hospital. His jeans were
stiff with salt and sand, only half-dry. Someone at the
emergency room must have lent him a plain green
scrub shirt, but his feet were still bare. His hair was
rumpled, his eyes exhausted.

And yet he was the most sublimely beautiful man
she had ever seen. Her throat closed over a sudden
wellspring of emotion. She couldn't even speak.

"He's going to be all right," Mark said quietly.
"They want to keep him overnight for observation.
And then tomorrow he'll check into a substance-abuse
center. He can't deny that he needs help any longer.
Not after tonight."

She nodded. "And emotionally? How are his spir-
its?"

He shook his head. "As you might expect. Tonight
was the worst, but he's been covering up a lot of pain
with the alcohol for a very long time. He'll have a lot
of work to do if he's going to live without it."

She nodded again. Poor Philip. She wondered
whether he had really wanted to die tonight, or
whether his confused brain had sent him into the water
searching for the girl he'd lost so long ago.

But she didn't want to ask. And what did it really
matter? Either way, it represented an unendurable level
of torment. She hoped that someday, with help, he
would find a way to come to terms with all of it.

"You saved his life, you know," Mark said suddenly. "You didn't have to, but you did. He's not in
any condition to thank you now. But I do, Glenna. I
thank you."

She flushed. "I didn't do anything," she protested.
"It was you—you and the doctors—"

"I was asleep, Glenna. I would never have known

he needed help if you hadn't warned me. You saved his life. It's as simple as that.'' He looked at her, a world of grief behind those tired, beautiful eyes. ''I wish...'' he said slowly, ''I wish I could have saved your sister. I wish I could bring her back to you now.''

She smiled shakily. ''I know,'' she said softly. ''I wish you could, too.''

''I *can* tell you what happened the night she died, though,'' he said gently. ''If you still want to hear about it.''

She raised her hand slightly, shrugging. ''Do you *want* to tell me?''

He rubbed his eyes with his thumb and forefinger. ''Yes,'' he said. ''I think perhaps I should.''

''All right, then,'' she agreed calmly. She waited while he seemed to collect his thoughts, as if he were wondering where to begin.

''Phil's been afraid of the water ever since he was a little boy. No one knows how it happened—he just hasn't ever been able to swim. It was tricky—living around here, being one of the Moonbird Connelly brothers. People pretty much expected him to be an aquatic superstar. Girls, especially. So he's had to pretend. He'll wade around a bit in the shallows, do some fancy skimboarding...things like that.''

Mark nudged a shell from its pocket of wet sand with a bare toe. Glenna looked at those long, well-proportioned feet and wondered why a bare foot should be so sensual.

''He thought your sister was the most exciting girl he'd ever met. When she asked him to take her out one night to hunt for the moonbird, he was thrilled. But when they got here, she wanted to go swimming. He didn't have the courage to tell her the truth, so he

agreed. He thought he could get by his usual way—
just dabbling a bit in the shallows.''

"But that wasn't enough for Cindy, was it?"
Glenna could almost picture the scene. Cindy loved to
swim—and she loved danger. She would never have
settled for a tame wade out to waist level.

"Apparently not. Philip says she just kept going
deeper. He couldn't stop her and he couldn't follow.
When she reached the sandbar, she tried to get him to
join her there, but he simply couldn't do it.''

Glenna suddenly appreciated the restraint with
which Mark was telling this story. She could all too
easily imagine how Cindy might have teased Philip.
Glenna herself had been labeled a chicken by her fear-
less older sister often enough to remember how it felt.

"Philip doesn't know what happened next. I think,
from his description, that it may have been a riptide.''
His voice was strained, as if he had come to the part
that would be most difficult to tell. "Riptides occur
around a gap in the sandbar—and they can be very
strong, difficult even for experienced swimmers to resist. Philip says there was very little warning. She just
seemed to disappear.''

*Oh, Cindy*... Glenna's heart ached. The golden girl
who had never known fear...

"Philip panicked. He waited a few minutes, hoping
she would resurface. Then he ran to get Edgerton.''

"Edgerton?''

"Yes. It wasn't quite as crazy as it sounds. Edge is
a superb swimmer. He'd spent all his summers life-
guarding. Anyhow, they both searched until well after
dawn. By then, they said, it was obviously too late.''

He sighed heavily, and she knew they were both
thinking that someone should have called the para-

medics as she had done tonight. How could anyone ever really know that it was too late?

"Edge says now that Philip really lost it, went a little nuts. Edgerton decided they shouldn't tell anyone because he thought Phil couldn't take the pressure of an inquiry." Mark shook his head. "I suspect he also hoped to avoid a family scandal. He was set to marry Deanna that summer, and her family would have been horrified."

"What about you?" She felt slightly weak. She wished there was somewhere to sit. "Did you think a cover-up was the best solution?"

"They didn't tell me." He sounded very tired again suddenly. "I had a reputation for being somewhat... indifferent...to public opinion. They decided they couldn't trust me to keep the secret. So they concocted an alibi for Philip, just in case Cindy had mentioned her assignation to anyone. They agreed to say he and Edgerton were together all night." He shook his head slowly. "The ironic thing about that was...when someone reported having seen a Connelly boy with Cindy that night, the only Connelly boy without an alibi was me."

She looked at him miserably. "Mark," she said, "I'm so sorry."

"It doesn't matter." He squatted down, picked up the shell he had unearthed and washed it in the edge of the surf. "They would have thought I was the most likely culprit anyhow. I was the black sheep, you know. The boy whose father was a criminal. The boy who didn't care what anyone said about him." He stood and twirled the shell thoughtfully, flipping it through his fingers with a slow, pensive rhythm. "But that part doesn't matter. I just wanted you to hear what really happened. I thought that, in some way, it might help for you to know.''

"How did you find out?'' She was mesmerized by the flash of the shell as it rotated in his hand. "*When* did you find out?''

"Last night.'' He flicked her a hard glance. "After I left your room, I corralled the two of them and told them what you had said. I told them...'' He looked away. "Well, anyway, I was...adamant.''

Glenna shuddered, imagining what kind of black fury lay behind that word.

"They wriggled around a little,'' he said, "but they knew they were hooked. Finally they came clean.''

"Were you going to tell me?'' she asked, careful to keep her tone guarded. This was dangerous ground. "Before—'' she waved her hand "—before all this happened, I mean.''

"Of course I was,'' he said as if he couldn't believe the question was serious. "Edgerton asked me to give him thirty-six hours. He wanted to tell Deanna and he wanted to withdraw gracefully from the legislative race. That seemed fair, so I agreed not to tell you until noon today.''

"Edgerton has withdrawn?'' She was stunned. "Why?''

He shot her a skeptical look. "Well, once the authorities are notified...it would be naive to think his candidacy could survive the scandal.''

"Oh. I see.'' She looked down where the rising sun, though still weak, was beginning to pick out glinting silver lights in the sand. "And you feel quite sure I'm going to tell the authorities, don't you?''

"Well...I was sure,'' he said slowly. "Until tonight.''

"And now?"

"And now I'm not sure what to think." He was frowning. The stubble of beard that had grown overnight made him look just slightly dangerous. "You had a chance to exact the perfect payment here tonight. An eye for an eye, so to speak. But you never even seemed to consider letting that happen. You were as determined to save Philip as I was."

She watched him silently, hoping against hope that his anger toward her might have softened. She would save a hundred cousins if she thought it might offset her sin of doubting him.

"It doesn't matter anyway," he said wearily. "You can go to the police if you like. Philip is too far gone right now to care. And Edgerton is relieved, I think, to have it finally all out in the open. I suspect it was harder living with that terrible, guilty secret than either of them ever imagined it would be." He fixed her with a solemn gaze. "Do whatever you think you must, Glenna. God knows you have the right. No one will blame you. *I* won't blame you."

She didn't answer. She couldn't. She could hear the emotional distance he was putting between them. It was as if he was building a wall one word at a time. It was over. He wasn't ever going to forgive her. It was so unfair. She would have forgiven him anything. Anything.

He took a step away. "I saw your suitcases in the lobby. I assume that means you're leaving this morning?"

As she nodded, his demeanor took on that of a courteous host. The slowly emerging dawn painted him an exhausted gray. He was as much a pale reflection of himself as that fading disk hanging in the ever-lightening sky was a pale reflection of the moon.

"I see. All right. Well, Deanna said she'd like to say goodbye. If you have time, perhaps you could speak to Amy, too." He turned, preparing to go.

"Wait," she cried, unable to stop herself. She reached out and touched his arm. "Don't leave everything like this, Mark. There's so much we haven't said. We've talked about the past until it's more real than the present. We know all about Cindy and we know all about Philip. But what about now? What about *us*?"

"Us?" He half turned so that she saw only his profile. It was stern, unyielding. "How can there be an us? The Connellys were responsible for your sister's death just as you always believed they were. This name, this place..." He held out his wrist where the moonbird was just visible in the growing light. "This *hand*. They're the stuff of your nightmares. Nothing I do can change that now."

He sounded so immovable, so resigned and implacable, that she thought her heart would break all over again. She felt the helpless tears pricking at her lids.

"There is only one nightmare left for me," she said, her voice trembling, on the verge of shattering, just as the wineglass had teetered at the edge of his roof the other night, on the brink of its destruction. "That is the nightmare in which you leave me. The one in which I have to go on living without you."

The abyss of that nightmare opened before her now, and she felt the ridiculous tears begin to flow. She didn't want to cry. She wanted to be mature, eloquent, persuasive, sophisticated. She wanted to make him see, understand, *believe*. She wanted his love, not his pity.

"I did trust you, Mark. I didn't *know* anything, but I *believed*. I believed in you. I believed in my love for you."

Her voice held up, but she couldn't stop the tears. They ran down her cheeks like a baby's tears, and when he saw them he let loose a deep, terrible curse.

"No," he said, reaching out to touch them, wipe them away as if he could force her to uncry them. "You must not. I can't bear it. I swore I'd never see you cry again."

"Then please," she said brokenly. "Stay with me."

"Why?" He sounded so cold. "You can't still love me after all of this."

"I do," she said wretchedly. "I will always love you. I won't be going to the police, Mark. I don't want what happened to ruin any more lives. I don't want it to have ruined *us*." She leaned her cheek into his hand. "Oh, Mark…can't you love me just a little?"

His whole body seemed frozen for a long, hard moment. Then he shook his head roughly, searching her gaze with eyes of flame. "No, God help me, Glenna, I can't."

She felt a piercing lightning strike of pure, undiluted despair. *He can't….*

And then he pulled her into his arms so hard she lost her balance. It was restored in an instant against the strength of his chest. The panic fluttered and flew away, replaced by a rush of the sweetest, purest hope.

"I can't love you just a little, sweetheart." He lowered his head so that his lips were only inches from hers. "I can only love you with all my heart."

"Mark—"

He kissed her, silencing her with a hard, unequivocal possession. Her body leaped to life. She leaned into him, molding herself to all the parts of him that were made for her, trying to believe that this was real, that this much happiness could last.

When he lifted his head, it was as if the nectar he had drunk from her lips had doused the terrible pain. His eyes were once again full of tenderness and laughter.

"I can only love you like this, Glenna. Wildly. Insanely. Completely."

She smiled through her tears. "Well…that might be enough," she said tremulously, hiccupping slightly. "Does that include breakfast? Lunch? And dinner?"

"Don't forget midnight snacks, too," he said, one corner of his mouth dimpling in a sinfully seductive way. "They're quite useful when you're having trouble sleeping."

She felt her heart beating up around her throat. It was too good to be true. "Edgerton warned me that you'd never settle for plain vanilla, Mark." She watched his face. She had to know if Edgerton had been right. "He said you'd never give up the more exotic flavors."

Mark laughed, and the sound was wonderful. "What would Edgerton know about what I want?"

He kissed her ear, running the tip of his nose along the soft outer ridge. Rays of shimmering heat sizzled out from the point of connection all the way into her abdomen. She shivered, thrilled to silence.

"In a way, he's right, though. I do need a lot of different flavors. I need flavors like laughter and loyalty. Like passion and pride. Like obstinacy and creativity and vulnerability and courage." He smiled. "I'll need all those flavors wrapped up in one tiny multicolored package." He brushed a kiss across her nose. "So don't change a bit, my love, no matter what Edgerton says. Keep a little of that virginal vanilla just for me. Who knows—from time to time, I may even need a taste of my fine old puritan panty hose pistachio."

"Oh, my goodness." She blushed complacently. "I honestly don't think Edgerton would recognize me in any of those descriptions. I'm not sure *I* recognize me."

He smiled. "Of course not. Purcell told me early on that what you don't know about yourself would fill an encyclopedia." He put a finger over her lips to silence her indignant protest. "And Edgerton's palate is not nearly educated enough to appreciate such a subtle blend of flavors. Which, my love, is why you're going to be my wife and not his."

"Your wife?" She caught his arms under suddenly trembling fingers.

"Yes, sweetheart," he said softly. "If you'll have me."

"But Deanna said that marriage wasn't in the Connelly nature."

"Deanna said? Edgerton said?" He shook her slightly, laughing. "No wonder we've had so much trouble getting this relationship straight. If you're going to take your romantic advice from *them*, my love, we're going to have a very rocky time of it." He stroked her upper arms sensuously, but his eyes were serious. "In the future, if you want to know something about me, you'll ask *me*, do you understand? *Only me*."

"Yes, sir," she said solemnly, as those long, strong fingers trailed pleasure across her skin. She finally knew that he had really forgiven her for doubting him.

And she knew that she would never do it again. "I'll make a note of it. Have question…ask Mark."

"Good. Now, as I was saying, if you'll marry me, I'll take you away from this place, away from these memories. We'll travel the world. We'll see beautiful places…you'll take beautiful pictures. And when we've found the most splendid spot on this whole splendid planet, then we'll build a home right there. And we'll raise our children there."

"What about the Moonbird?" She frowned, glancing back at the hotel, which lay quiet and gray in the early-morning light. "You told me once that after you've loved her in the moonlight, nothing else will ever do."

"That's right," he said, smiling. "You see, she's very beautiful in the moonlight, my little moonbird.…"

He kissed her again, this time with an exquisite tenderness. She sank eagerly into his arms, expecting fire, prepared for passion. But what she got instead was a strange sense of overwhelming peace, as if they had entered a special world where enchantment ruled, where all problems evaporated magically under the soft glow of moonlight.

The air was suddenly intensely sweet. Her skin tingled all over. She had the oddest sense that Cindy might be watching somewhere, smiling.

"Mark," she whispered against his lips, wondering if he felt this extraordinary peace, too.

"I know," he answered softly. "This is how it feels, my love, when the dawn has finally come."

She stopped wondering then and gave herself up to the feeling. Time stretched. A little later—minutes, perhaps, or maybe only seconds—they heard a soft

# Take 4 bestselling love stories FREE

## Plus get a FREE surprise gift!

# Catch more great

## HARLEQUIN™ Movies

**featured on** the movie channel tmc

### Premiering May 9th
### *The Awakening*

starring Cynthia Geary and
David Beecroft, based on the novel by
Patricia Coughlin

Don't miss next month's movie!
Premiering June 13th
*Diamond Girl*
based on the novel by bestselling author
Diana Palmer

If you are not currently a subscriber to
The Movie Channel, simply call your
local cable or satellite provider for more
details. Call today, and don't miss out
on the romance!

the movie channel tmc

HARLEQUIN®
*Makes any time special* ™

*100% pure movies.*
*100% pure fun.*

# *Presents Extravaganza*
# 25 YEARS!

**With the purchase of two Harlequin Presents®
books, you can send in for a FREE Silvertone Book
Pendant. Retail value $19.95. It's our gift to you!**

## FREE SILVERTONE BOOK PENDANT

On the official proof-of-purchase coupon below, fill in your name,
address and zip or postal code, and send it, plus $1.50 U.S./
$2.50 CAN. for postage and handling, (check or money order—please
do not send cash), to Harlequin books: In the U.S.: 3010 Walden
Avenue, P.O. Box 9077, Buffalo, N.Y. 14269-9077; In Canada: P.O. Box
609, Fort Erie, Ontario L2A 5X3. Please allow 4-6 weeks for delivery.
Order your Silvertone Book Pendant now! Quantities are limited. Offer
for the FREE Silvertone Book Pendant expires December 31, 1998.

# Coming Next Month

## HARLEQUIN PRESENTS®

### THE BEST HAS JUST GOTTEN BETTER!

**#1959 SINFUL PLEASURES Anne Mather**
Megan was back in San Felipe to find that much had changed.
Her stepsister's son, Remy, had been nine to her fifteen when
she saw him last—now he was a deeply attractive man. And
Megan sensed danger.

**#1960 THE MARRIAGE CAMPAIGN Helen Bianchin**
Dominic wanted Francesca, and he'd planned a very special
campaign for winning her. She may be wary of loving again,
but he was going to pursue, charm and seduce her
relentlessly—until she said yes!

**#1961 THE SECRET WIFE Lynne Graham**
Nothing could have prepared Rosie for Greek tycoon
Constantine Voulos—or his insistence that she marry him! But
she soon realized she couldn't just be his temporary wife. Her
secret would have to be told!

**#1962 THE DIVORCÉE SAID YES! Sandra Marton**
**(The Wedding of the Year)**
When Chase suggested to ex-wife, Annie, that they pretend to
get back together to reassure their daughter that love could
last, Annie was amazed. But then she found herself agreeing
to his plan....

**#1963 ULTIMATE TEMPTATION Sara Craven**
**(Nanny Wanted!)**
Count Giulio Falcone needed a nanny to look after his sister's
children. Lucy was in his debt *and* in his house. Suddenly she
found herself in the wrong place at the wrong time, with the
ultimate temptation—Giulio!

**#1964 GIRL TROUBLE Sandra Field**
**(Man Talk)**
Cade loved Lori, but she had two daughters—one of whom
had taken an instant dislike to him. He only wanted one
blonde in his life, not three. Trouble was, getting Lori into his
bed meant accepting the little girls into his heart!